Could he trust himself enough to try? Trust her? He wasn't sure.

What if she suddenly realised she wasn't as strong as she thought? What if it all fell apart and she found she couldn't take it and wanted out? If he let himself love her…

But if he didn't try, if he didn't let her try, then they'd lose it all anyway. Life had no guarantees.

'OK,' he said, feeling the ground fall away from under his feet. 'We'll try—but I'm not promising anything, Anita. I've never stuck at this in my life, and I'm thirty-five. That's a long time to spend moving on.'

'I know. And we'll take it step by step, and I won't put any pressure on you, I promise. Let's just see what happens.'

Her eyes were gentle, her face so close he only had to move his head a little way for their lips to touch.

She met him halfway, her breath easing over his face in a soft sigh as their lips met. With a ragged groan he gathered her into his arms and kissed her as if she was the most precious thing he'd ever held, and deep inside her she felt a glimmer of hope spring to life.

She knew he loved her. All she had to do was wait for him to realise it, too…

Dear Reader

A few years ago I wrote a book, THE VALTIERI MARRIAGE DEAL, about a scrummy Italian doctor called Luca Valtieri. He had two brothers, equally gorgeous, who since then have clamoured for their own books. Massimo (VALTIERI'S BRIDE), a widower with three adorable children, was the eldest of the family, and Gio, a lawyer, was the youngest brother. They had a family friend, Anita, who planned Luca's wedding and then Massimo's, and I thought, What better than to match her up with Gio?

He's cynical, wary, commitment-phobic, and Anita has loved him her entire life. A wedding planner, she's deeply romantic and has been waiting years for him to realise that he loves her. But there's a tragedy lurking in his past—something he's never told her—and it's keeping them apart.

And then he's injured as a result of an attack, and she looks after him. They're thrown together, and there's no escape as they travel the passionate and emotional rollercoaster that ensues.

I've loved every one of these brothers, but Gio, for me, has a special place in my heart. I hope you find a place for him, too, as you travel their rollercoaster with them.

Love

Caroline

If you would like to catch up with Caroline Anderson's other stories featuring the Valtieri family
THE VALTIERI MARRIAGE DEAL
from Mills & Boon® Medical™ Romance and
VALTIERI'S BRIDE from Mills & Boon® Cherish™
visit www.millsandboon.co.uk where they are
available in eBook format

THE VALTIERI BABY

BY
CAROLINE ANDERSON

First published in Great Britain 2012
by Mills & Boon, an imprint of Harlequin (UK) Limited.
Harlequin (UK) Limited, Eton House, 18-24 Paradise Road,
Richmond, Surrey TW9 1SR

© Caroline Anderson 2012

ISBN: 978 0 263 22793 2

Harlequin (UK) policy is to use papers that are natural, renewable
and recyclable products and made from wood grown in sustainable
forests. The logging and manufacturing process conform to the
legal environmental regulations of the country of origin.

Printed and bound in Great Britain
by CPI Antony Rowe,

Caroline Anderson has the mind of a butterfly. She's been a nurse, a secretary, a teacher, run her own soft furnishing business, and now she's settled on writing. She says, 'I was looking for that elusive something. I finally realised it was variety, and now I have it in abundance. Every book brings new horizons and new friends, and in between books I have learned to be a juggler. My teacher husband, John, and I have two beautiful and talented daughters, Sarah and Hannah, umpteen pets, and several acres of Suffolk that nature tries to reclaim every time we turn our backs!' Caroline also writes for the Mills & Boon® Medical™ Romance series.

Books by Caroline Anderson:

VALTIERI'S BRIDE
THE BABY SWAP MIRACLE
MOTHER OF THE BRIDE
THE VALTIERI MARRIAGE DEAL*

*Published in the
 Mills & Boon® Medical™ Romance series.

Did you know these are also available as eBooks?
Visit www.millsandboon.co.uk

For my husband, John, my daughters,
Sarah and Hannah, and my grandson, Maximus,
who underline for me on a daily basis
how precious and important family is.
I love you.

CHAPTER ONE

'SIGNORE Valtieri! Wait! Please, Signore, listen to me!'

Her distraught voice sliced through the evening shadows, and Gio's heart sank. Not now, he thought. Please, not now. He really, *really* didn't have the energy to deal with Camilla Ponti diplomatically, and he certainly didn't have the time.

He'd already stalled his holiday once because of her, and he wasn't doing it again.

She'd been about to take action against his client, Marco Renaldo, but Marco had insisted on talking to her before the case came to court. Gio had postponed his departure for a day so they could meet this afternoon, and she'd dropped her claim.

Not quietly.

She'd sobbed and begged and pleaded, but her former business partner had left her no choice. Drop the case, or he'd reveal her fraud and embezzlement of the company's funds. She'd given in, but she'd blamed Gio for putting him up to it, because she was convinced he'd cost her her share of the company.

It was absurd. She'd forfeited any rights to it herself. He couldn't believe she'd even thought she had a case! The meeting over, he'd sent a text to Anita arranging to pick her up at six, then, more than ready to get out of the city, he'd gone home and stripped off the exquisitely cut suit, the tasteful silk tie Anita had given him for Christmas, the blinding white shirt. He'd put away the immaculate hand-made shoes, the monogrammed cufflinks, also from Anita, and showered and pulled on his favourite jeans and sweater, the battered leather jacket and boots that had seen better days.

Then he'd pulled the refuse bag out of the kitchen waste bin, flung in the remnants of food from the fridge, tossed an empty wine bottle in on top and headed for the door.

He couldn't get out of Firenze and away from all this quick enough. His luggage was in the car, and he was looking forward to two weeks on the slopes with his family skiing, eating, and thinking about precisely nothing.

Except Anita would be there. Just thinking about it sent a tingle of anticipation through his veins. He'd missed her recently. He'd been avoiding her ever since the night of his brother's wedding when things had got a little complicated—again—but at least with his whole family present there'd be plenty of people to diffuse the tension, and he knew a huge part of the attraction of this holiday was that she'd be there.

He couldn't get there soon enough. For some reason, the cut and thrust of his job had lost its lustre recently, and after a day like today he just felt tired and jaded.

And now this.

This woman, who'd somehow found out where he lived and was lying in wait so she could carry on their earlier conversation. Frankly, he'd heard enough.

'Signora Ponti, there is really nothing more to say,' he began, groping for diplomacy, but it was wasted on her.

'You don't understand! You have to help me—please, listen to me! I need the money—'

'Signora, everyone needs money, but you can't just have it if it isn't yours, and as Signore Renaldo pointed out, you've already stolen more than enough from him—'

'It wasn't like that! I had reasons—'

'Everyone has reasons,' he said tiredly. 'Now, if you'll excuse me, I'm meeting someone and I'm already late.'

'But I *earned* that money, I really need it,' she sobbed, reaching for him with desperate hands. 'Please, you have to listen!'

He stepped back out of reach, his patience exhausted. 'No, I don't. I've heard enough,' he said flatly, and started to turn away, the bag of refuse still in his hand.

'Nooooooo!'

Out of the corner of his eye he saw her raise her arm, but it was too late to duck. His free arm was still coming up to shield his face when something large and heavy— her handbag?—crashed into his head and sent him reeling. He tripped over the edge of the kerb, twisting his ankle sharply, the pain sickening. It gave way under him, throwing him further off balance, and he felt himself falling.

He couldn't save himself.

He dropped the refuse bag, heard the tinkling sound of broken glass just too late to roll to the side, and then a sharp, searing pain in his thigh took his breath away.

On autopilot, still waiting for another blow to fall, he rolled off the bag and glared at her, but she was so distraught that he'd never be able to reason with her. It was pointless trying.

For a long moment he lay there, shocked, his eyes locked with hers, but then he became aware of something hot and wet dripping off his fingers, and he stared blankly at his hand, and then his thigh, and he realised he was in trouble.

So did she, her face crumpling as she took in what had happened.

'No! No—I'm so sorry! I didn't mean to hurt you! Please—oh, no…!'

And turning on her heel, she ran away, leaving him there alone in the dim light of the car park, the sound of her high heels rapping sharply on the stones fading as she fled.

Relief sapping the last of his strength, he slumped back against the wall behind him and closed his eyes for a moment.

Dio, he hurt.

He looked down at his foot, bent at a strange angle. No, not his foot, he realised with relief. The boot, twisted half off where he'd tripped. But his foot was inside it and the pain was just beginning to break through all the other insults, so his relief was short-lived. Maybe not so good after all.

And there was glass sticking out of his leg. He knew he probably shouldn't pull it out, but his leg was bleeding and with the glass in there he couldn't put pressure on it, so he pulled it out anyway.

Not a good move, apparently.

Wrapping his scarf roughly around his slashed hand, he closed his fingers tight over it and rammed his fist hard down on his thigh, then rummaged for his phone. He'd call Anita. There was no point in calling either of his brothers, they and their families were already at the ski chalet, as were his sisters and his parents, but Anita was expecting him. She had a meeting with a bride and he was supposed to be picking her up any time now.

She'd help him. She always helped him, she'd always

known just what to do when he'd got himself in a mess. And she'd rescue him now. Relief coursing through him, his whole body shaking, his left hand struggling to cooperate, he speed-dialled her number.

It went straight to voicemail.

He listened to the message, heard the soft lilt of her voice and could have howled with frustration and despair.

'Why is it,' he said sarcastically when the cheery message finally ended, 'that I'm tripping over you all the time, and yet the one time I really need you you're not there?'

He cut off and watched the blood still slowly welling from his thigh for another few seconds before he did what he should have done in the first place. He called an ambulance.

And then he leant back against the wall behind him, and dialled her number again, and then again. He needed her, and he couldn't get her, but it was somehow comforting just to listen to the sound of her voice…

Her phone was ringing.

She could feel it in her pocket, vibrating silently as she wound up her meeting. It rang again. And again.

Damn. It would be Gio, wondering where she was. He'd be foaming at the mouth if she didn't go soon.

'Right, I think I've got all I need for now,' she told her client briskly. 'I'll go and put a few ideas together for you, and then we'll get back together again when I'm back from my holiday.'

'Oh—I was hoping we could do it all today…'

Anita's smile faltered as the phone vibrated again.

'I'm sorry, I'm already late. I'm supposed to be leaving for my holiday and I only fitted you in today because I was delayed, I should have gone yesterday. Don't worry, please, there'll be plenty of time to sort everything out. It's seven months to the wedding.'

She shut her file and stood up, effectively ending the meeting, and held out her hand to the bride.

The girl smiled reluctantly and got up, taking her hand. 'Sorry. I just want all the answers at once.'

'Everybody does. It's not possible, but it will happen. I'll see you in two weeks when I'm back from my holiday. I'll call you with a date.'

'OK. And—thank you for fitting me in. I'm sorry to be a pain.'

'You aren't a pain. I'll call you, I promise.'

And with one last brisk, professional smile she walked away, resisting the urge to pull her phone from her pocket before she'd left the café and was out of sight.

Six missed calls. *Six?*

And all from Gio. Damn. She really *was* late, and he'd be truly, no-holds-barred furious with her. He hated it when people were late.

Except he didn't sound furious. He sounded...

She listened to her voicemail message in puzzlement, and tried to call him.

It went straight to voicemail, again and again, but she couldn't give up, because something about his message was worrying her and she didn't know what it was.

'Why is it that I'm tripping over you all the time, and yet the one time I really need you you're not there?'

Anita frowned, and played it again. Far from angry, his voice sounded odd. Odd, and slightly desperate. As if he was in trouble—

Her heart pounding now, she tried him again, and this time the phone was answered by a stranger.

'Hello? Are you Anita?'

'Yes—Anita Della Rossa. Where's Gio? Who are you?'

'This is a nurse in the emergency department...'

She didn't hear the rest. For a second, all she could hear was roaring in her ears from the frantic beating of her heart.

'I knew there was something wrong, I've been trying to get hold of him. What's happened to him?' she asked, desperate for information. 'Did he have an accident? Is he all right?'

'Are you family?'

She nearly lied, but there was no point, they were all too well known. 'No, but I'm an old family friend. I've known him forever.' Her voice cracked, and she tried again. 'They're all away—they've gone skiing. We were about to join them. Please, tell me how he is.'

'He's had an accident and he's going to surgery. That's all I can tell you. Can you give us his full name and family contact details, please? We need to ring them urgently.'

Urgently? Her heart lurched in her chest, and for a second she thought she was going to be sick.

'Um—yes—he's Giovanni Valtieri. His brother Luca's a doctor at the hospital—a professor. Contact him. He's with the others.' She gave them Luca's number just to be certain, then raced to the hospital, her heart in her mouth. But in the hospital emergency department she met another brick wall, built, no doubt, by the same protocol.

'I spoke to a nurse,' she explained. 'I was calling Giovanni Valtieri, and the person who answered his phone said he was here. Can I see him?'

'Are you family?'

Yet again, she thought of lying, but it was pointless, so she just trowelled on the connection. 'No, but I'm an old family friend. We've been very close since we were born—almost like brother and sister.'

And ex-lovers, she nearly added, but that was nobody else's business and she wasn't going to spread something so personal all over the hospital. Not when his brother worked there.

So they wouldn't tell her any more, but that was fine. There were strings she could pull, and she fully intended to pull every single one of them. Starting with Luca...

He felt like hell.

He lay there for a moment, assessing his body. It was throbbing, and after a bit the throbbing separated out so he could catalogue it.

His right hand hurt. He tried to flex his fingers, but it didn't seem like a good idea and anyway his hand seemed to be heavily bandaged.

OK. Right thigh—well, that certainly hurt, with a deep ache close up by his groin, but thankfully not *that* close.

And his right foot. They'd cut his jeans off to get to his leg, and they'd wanted to cut the boot off—his favourite boots. It had taken ages to break them in like that. He'd refused to let them, vaguely detached from it all through loss of blood. Until they'd eased it off. He hadn't been detached then, and the last thing he remembered was the sickening pain. He must have passed out at that point.

And he had a killer headache. He frowned. She hadn't touched his head, but maybe when he'd fallen he'd cracked it on the wall behind him. Either that or she'd had a rock in that ludicrous bag.

He breathed in, caught the hint of a familiar scent and his eyes flew open, searching for her.

'Anita?'

She came into view, her warm brown eyes troubled. She was smiling, but there was a slight tremor in her lips, and she was pale. He'd never seen anything more beautiful in his life.

'*Ciao,* Gio,' she murmured, leaning over him to brush a kiss against his cheek. 'How are you feeling?'

'Fine,' he lied, but she just snorted and raised a slender, disbelieving eyebrow a fraction.

'I am. Of course I'm all right.'

'Well, you don't look it. You look like you've been partying with the vampires.'

'Very funny,' he said, turning away so he didn't have to see the worried look in her eyes.

'I called Luca,' she said, and he snapped his head back round again.

'You *what*?'

'I called Luca. They wouldn't tell me anything, wouldn't let me in to see you, so I pulled strings.'

Damn. 'What did he say?'

'He's threatening to come back.'

'That's ridiculous! It's just a scratch—'

'Gio, you don't get taken into Theatre for a scratch!'

She broke off, took a breath and then carried on in a level tone, 'Anyway, your mother snatched the phone off him before he could say much and she's pretty upset. I promised I'd get you to ring her the moment you came round.'

He let out a short, harsh sigh and closed his eyes.

He shouldn't have called her—except, of course, he would have had to because he was supposed to have been picking her up *en route*. And when he didn't turn up and she couldn't get him, she would have rung alarm bells anyway.

'You shouldn't have called him.'

'They already had. They asked me for family contact details, and they wouldn't tell me anything so I had no idea how badly you'd been hurt, but it sounded bad. They used the word "urgent",' she said drily. 'It didn't seem like the time to argue.'

No, of course not. What was he thinking? The moment he'd been admitted and they found out his identity they would have been on the phone to his brother, because he worked in the hospital and was known to all of them.

And now apparently Luca was threatening to come back and his mother was in hysterics and all because some stupid, *stupid* woman had come after him.

'So—what actually happened?' she asked, perching on the edge of the chair beside him and reaching for his hand, then thinking better of it because of the bandages.

'A client's ex-business partner hit me with her handbag,' he said, his voice disgusted, and she gave a tiny incredulous laugh.

'Excuse me? Her *what*?'

'Humiliating, isn't it,' he said drily, 'but it gets worse. I ducked out of the way, tripped over the kerb and fell over my own refuse bag. That'll teach me to do my recycling properly.'

Anita glared at him. 'Gio, how can you joke about it? They told me it was serious! What really happened?'

He gave a short, dry laugh. 'That is exactly what happened, and believe me, it feels pretty serious. I hurt like hell.'

'I can imagine.' She bit her lip, puzzled. She still hadn't got to the bottom of this, she was sure. 'So—what did she *actually* do to you? Really?'

'Apart from attempting to knock me out with her

handbag? Nothing. She didn't need to. Goodness knows what she keeps in it, the thing weighed a ton. Anyway, it knocked me off balance and I fell over the refuse bag. Then I pulled the glass out. Not a smart move.'

She rolled her eyes, then frowned, sifting through his words again and coming up with something she didn't understand. 'What glass, Gio? Pulled it out of *what*?'

'I reckon it was a wine bottle. I dropped the bag, and I heard glass breaking before I fell on it. I cut my hand when I fell, and a piece stuck in my thigh, so I pulled it out, but it wasn't a good idea because it had severed the artery. If it happens again, apparently, I have to leave it there. Don't worry, it missed the important bits,' he added drily.

She glared at him, shocked he'd been hurt so badly and furious that he was treating it so lightly when she'd been going through hell. 'This is no time for joking, Gio! A severed artery? You could have bled to death!'

He reached out his hand, then remembered and dropped it carefully back onto the covers.

'Come round this side,' he said gruffly, but there was a drip there and it was no better.

Actually, that wasn't true. It was better. She sat down beside him, threaded her shaking fingers carefully through his and closed them firmly round his hand.

Dio, it felt good to hold her. The warmth from her palm spread into him and thawed the ice that seemed to have formed inside him, and as the tension eased, he realised how tight he'd been holding himself.

For a moment they said nothing, then she frowned slightly, her brow puckering as she tried to make sense of it.

'Why did she try to attack you, Gio? Who was she? One of your thwarted lovers?'

He laughed softly. 'No. A very disappointed woman. We had a meeting with her today, the reason I had to delay leaving, and she came off worst. She feels I cheated her.'

'And did you?'

'No. I just made sure she got what she deserved from my client, which was nothing,' he said, and he watched her frown again.

'Wow. And she attacked you for that?'

'Well, to be fair I did most of it myself when I fell up the kerb and landed on the bag. Apparently my ankle isn't broken, though, which is good news. It's just bruised and sprained.'

He nearly laughed at the 'just' but he hurt too much to bother.

'And your hand?' she asked, arching a brow towards his bandaged fingers. 'I can still see all your fingers, so I guess you didn't cut them off.'

'No. They seem to be there and they all move. As I say, most of it was my own fault.'

'Mmm. That really wasn't very clever, was it?'

He snorted at the mild understatement, and her fingers tightened a little. 'Sorry. The police are here, by the way, waiting for you to feel well enough to talk to them. And you need to phone your mother.'

He nodded. 'Call her now for me—I'll talk to her first. And then I'll talk to the police. She didn't really do anything.'

'Gio, she attacked you. If she hadn't, none of this would have happened.'

'She hit me with her handbag. That's all. The police don't need to be involved.'

'And if she comes after you again?'

He shrugged. 'She won't. And if she does, I'll be ready for her this time.'

She gave up arguing. She dialled his mother, handed him the phone and then left him alone and went and found something to eat and drink.

It could have been fantastic, or cardboard. It wouldn't have made any difference, because she couldn't taste it, not with the image of him lying there like a ghost so fresh in her mind. But it was food, and she ate it mechanically while she beat herself up about not answering his first call.

What if he'd died? What if he'd rung her, and then passed out from loss of blood before he could call an ambulance? No, he must have called one first. He surely wouldn't have been stupid enough to call her so many times before he called the medical services? Maybe, if he had her on speed-dial. Maybe he'd thought it would be quicker, but then she hadn't answered, and that could have cost him his life…

She felt sick, and pushed away the last of her panini. Cardboard, she decided finally, realising she was probably being unfair, but whatever, she couldn't eat any more of it. She went back to him, and found him propped up on his pillows looking pale and drawn and very tired.

'What did the police say?'

'They're going to talk to her. Apparently she called an ambulance, so she at least has a conscience, but her phone's now switched off—'

'She called an ambulance?'

'Yes—why?'

Because it meant he wouldn't have died because of her. She shook her head, relief taking her legs out from under her, so she sat down shakily on the chair beside him. 'Nothing. I'm just surprised. So how are you feeling?'

He shrugged. 'Much the same. The doctor's been, as well, while you were gone. They're going to keep me in overnight and review me in the morning, but they think I can probably go home tomorrow. I have to have another blood transfusion. The vampires were a bit greedy.'

He smiled, but she couldn't smile back. Not when he'd come so close. She looked at her watch. Nearly midnight.

'I'll go home now, then, and I'll come back in the morning. Do you want me to bring you some clothes in when I come?'

'Please. My bags are in the car already. If you could bring the small one, it's got everything I'll need. The big one's just ski stuff. You'd better clear it with the police on the way out, or they might not let you get it. It'll be a crime scene now, apparently. I've told them they're over-reacting, but they seem to feel they need to collect the evidence. Here, my keys. It's the little Mercedes sports, by the way.'

'Where's the Ferrari?'

He smiled. 'I do too much driving in the city. It was fun, but not practical in the city streets. The Mercedes is much more sensible.'

'That doesn't sound like you.'

'Maybe I've changed.'

She just laughed at that. Giovanni Valtieri would never change. She'd given up hoping for miracles.

She took the keys from him, and bent and kissed his cheek, letting her face rest there for a moment. She could feel the slight rasp of stubble, the roughness curiously comforting and reassuring as he turned his head against hers and touched her cheek with his lips.

'I'll see you in the morning,' she murmured, and with another light brush of her lips against his jaw she straightened up and met his dark, weary eyes.

'*Ciao,* Anita,' he mumbled tiredly. 'And thank you.'

'*Prego.* You take care. No more fighting with women.'

He gave a soft chuckle and raised his good hand as she left, and she winked at him and went out into the corridor. The policeman was there, and she asked him to contact the team at his apartment building to alert them that she'd need access to his car.

Then she walked away without waiting for the OK. She was tired and emotionally exhausted, and she just wanted to get home, but first she had to get his bag. The area was cordoned off by the police, as he'd said, and she had to get them to escort her to his car and get the soft leather grip from it.

She made her way home, undressed and crawled into bed, but she couldn't sleep. She could so easily have lost him—not that he was hers anyway, but the thought of him dying—

'No! Stop it! He's going to be all right. Stop torturing yourself.'

But all she could see was his washed-out face.

'So can you go?'

'Yes, but I have no idea *where* I'm supposed to go. I can't drive like this, I can't get upstairs to my apartment, and the police have said it's not a good idea to go back to my apartment anyway until they've spoken to Camilla Ponti and assessed her state of mind, but they can't find her anywhere. She wasn't at her home address or any of the other places they've tried, and they just don't think it's a good idea for me to hang around in Firenze.'

She nodded. That made sense.

'So why not go on holiday as we'd planned? I can drive.'

'On a skiing holiday? What's the point? I won't be able

to do anything. You go and join the others, I'll just go home to the *palazzo*. Carlotta can look after me.'

She shook her head. 'They're away. They've gone to visit their grandchildren in Napoli while your family don't need them. There's no one there.'

Damn. He'd forgotten that. So what was he supposed to do?

'Well, you'd better come with me, then,' she said after a slight pause. 'I'm on holiday now, so are you—we'll go to my villa, and I can look after you.'

'No. You're supposed to be going skiing. You can't do that for me,' he objected, ludicrously tempted.

'Why on earth not? I've been rescuing you since you learned to climb trees. Why not now? You can't cook, you can't walk, you can't drive, but you can rest and recover there while you keep out of the way and wait for the police to catch her. It's the obvious solution.'

It was. So obvious he'd already thought of it and dismissed it. On the surface it sounded the perfect plan. The only 'but'—and it was a huge one—was that it meant spending the next two weeks with Anita alone, with no one to diffuse the tension.

And that was a *bad* idea.

CHAPTER TWO

It took them a while to discharge him, but finally he was wheeled to the entrance.

Anita's car was there, drawn up to the kerb, engine running. All he had to do was get out of the wheelchair and into it.

Huh. It was a nightmare, but he gritted his teeth and managed somehow. His inflexible right foot in its support bandage was the most awkward thing—that, and the fact that his wounded thigh muscles really didn't want to lift his leg, and his heavily bandaged right hand was all but useless.

It didn't help that it was tipping down with rain, either, but at last he was in, more or less dry with the help of a man with an umbrella, and the door was shut.

'OK?' she asked briskly as he was finally settled beside her, but he'd known her nearly thirty-five years, and the concern in her voice was obvious to him.

Obvious, and strangely reassuring.

'I'm fine,' he lied through gritted teeth. 'Just get us out of here.'

He turned up the collar of his rain-spattered and blood-stained leather jacket and hunched down in the seat as she pulled away. He was glad to be getting out of the city.

He didn't think Camilla Ponti posed a real threat, but the last thing he wanted was Anita in danger, however slight the risk.

She left the city streets behind, heading out of Firenze, and after a few minutes she turned her head and flashed him a smile. 'Better now?'

They were on the A1 heading south past Siena towards the Montalcino area where both his family and hers had lived for generations.

Home, he thought with a sigh of relief.

'Much better,' he said, and resting his head back on the seat, he closed his eyes and drifted off.

He was asleep.

Good. He'd lost a lot of blood, and he'd be exhausted. She didn't suppose he'd slept much last night, what with the pain and awkwardness of his injuries, and anyway, it was easier for her if he wasn't watching her while she drove, because his presence, familiar as it was, always scrambled her brains.

Even when he was fast asleep she was ludicrously conscious of him, deeply, desperately aware of every breath, every sigh, every slight shift of his solid, muscular body.

She knew every inch of it. Loved every inch of it. Always had, always would.

Fruitlessly, of course. The one time she'd felt there was any hope for them it had been snatched away abruptly and without warning, and left her heart in tatters. Anyone with any sense would walk away from him, tell him to go to hell and find his own solution, but Anita couldn't do that.

She couldn't walk away from him. Goodness knows she'd tried a hundred times, but her heart kept drawing her back because deep down she believed that he loved her, whatever he might say to the contrary.

And one day…

She gave a soft, sad huff of laughter. One day nothing. She was stupid, deluded, desperate.

'Hey.'

She turned her head and met his eyes briefly, then dragged hers back to the road.

'How are you?' she asked. 'Good sleep?'

'I'm just resting.'

'You were snoring.'

'I don't snore.'

'You do.' He did. Not loudly, not much, just a soft sound that was curiously comforting beside her. As it had been, for those few blissful weeks five years ago.

'Why did you laugh?'

'Laugh?' She hadn't—

'Yes, laugh. If you can call it that. You didn't look exactly amused.'

Ah. *That* laugh, the one that wasn't. The laugh because against all the odds she could still manage to believe he loved her.

'I was thinking about my meeting yesterday,' she lied. 'The bride thought we could wrap it all up in an hour. She was miffed when I left.'

'Is that where you were when I rang you?'

She nodded, biting her lip at the little rush of guilt, and he tilted his head and frowned.

'Anita? It wasn't your fault. I knew you were in a meeting.'

'I should have been out by then. I could have answered it—*should* have answered it.'

'I wouldn't have answered you if I'd been with a client.'

Of course not. She *knew* that, but it didn't make any difference, and if he'd died—

His hand closed over hers, squeezing gently. 'Hey, I'm all right,' he said softly. 'I was fine, and the ambulance came really quickly, because she'd already called it.'

'Well, good. I don't suppose there was a lot of time to waste, and what if she hadn't called it? What if you'd passed out?'

He dropped his hand again. 'It was fine, the bleeding was all under control,' he lied. 'And I'm all right, you can see that. Now I just have to get better. I wonder if they've found her yet.'

'Will she go to prison for it?'

He laughed a little grimly. 'What, for hitting me with her handbag? No. She didn't mean to do this, Anita.'

'You're very forgiving.'

'No, I'm not. I'm thoroughly peed off because I shouldn't even have been here, I should have been on holiday and the only reason I wasn't was because of her. I'm just a realist and anyway, it's not really me she's angry with, it's Marco. It's just profoundly irritating.'

Irritating? She nearly laughed. 'So, have you warned him? Your client? She might go after him.'

'Don't worry, he's out of the country now. He was leaving yesterday straight after our meeting, but anyway he has very good security.'

'Maybe you should move to somewhere more secure. Your apartment isn't exactly impenetrable. OK, she might be just a bit of a nutter, but what if it was someone really serious, with a real grudge?'

He shrugged, contemplating the idea not for the first time, but he loved it where he was, overlooking the rooftops. He had a fabulous view and he was loath to lose it.

Sometimes he sat out on his little roof terrace and imagined that the rolling hills there in the distance were home.

They weren't, he knew that, but sometimes he just had a yearning to be back there, and those distant hills made him feel closer. The idea of moving to some gated community or apartment complex with hefty security and nothing to look at through the windows but carefully manicured grounds brought him out in hives.

'I'll think about it,' he said, knowing full well he wouldn't, and he closed his eyes and listened to the rhythmic swish of the windscreen wipers as she drove him home.

He was asleep when she turned onto the long gravel drive that led to her villa.

It had once been the main dwelling on her family's farm, long superseded by a much larger villa, and she loved it. It was small and unpretentious, but it was hers, it had stunning views, and it was perfect for Gio's recovery because it was single storey and so he wouldn't have to struggle with stairs.

Her headlights raked the front of the villa, and she drew up outside and opened the door quietly, easing out of the car without disturbing him. She'd put the radio on quietly while he slept, and she left it on while she went in and turned up the heating.

It wasn't cold, exactly, but it was cheerless even though the rain had stopped now, and she pulled sheets out of the linen cupboard and quickly made up her spare bed for him. It was a good room, the view from the bed stretching miles into the distance, and on the top of the hill on the horizon was the Palazzo Valtieri, home to his family for hundreds of years.

The lights were off now, the *palazzo* deserted, but normally she could see it in the dark. It was quite distinctive, and at night the lights could be seen for miles. She'd lost count of the number of times she'd lain there in her bedroom next to this one and stared at them, wondering if he was there, if he was awake, if he was looking for the lights of her villa.

Probably not. Why would he? He didn't feel the same about her, he'd made that perfectly clear five years ago when he'd ended their relationship without warning. And anyway, most of the time he was in Firenze, where he lived and worked.

But still she looked, and wondered, and yearned.

'Stop it!' she muttered, and made the bed. Torturing herself with memories was pointless—as pointless as staring at the *palazzo* on the hill like a love-struck teenager night after night.

But she *felt* like a love-struck teenager, even after all this time. Nothing had changed—except now she didn't have to imagine what it felt like to lie in his arms, because she *knew*.

She tugged the quilt straight, turned it back so he could get in, and went outside, switching on the porch lights.

He was awake. She could tell that, even though his eyes were closed, and as she walked towards him, her boots crunching on the gravel, they opened and looked straight at her through the windscreen.

He didn't want to come in. She could tell that, just as she'd been able to tell he was awake. Well, that was fine. She didn't really want him to, either, because it meant keeping up an impossible charade of indifference for the next two weeks, and she really, really didn't know if she could do it.

But it seemed that neither of them had a choice.

* * *

He had to do it.

There was no point delaying it, he had to get out of the car and hobble into the house and try, somehow, not to remember the last time he'd been in there.

The night of his brother Massimo's wedding, nine months ago.

Long enough to make a baby.

That was a random thought. And if he hadn't stopped, if he hadn't walked away and got back in his car and driven back to Firenze, they might have done just that.

They'd had a great day. A quiet family wedding, with a simple ceremony in the town hall followed by a meal in a restaurant owned by a member of their housekeeper Carlotta's family.

And then Massimo had taken his bride home, and the rest of them had ended up at Luca's with all the children. Too much for him, and too much for Anita, so he'd given her a lift home, and she'd offered him coffee before he headed back to Firenze, and he'd accepted.

Except they'd never got as far as the coffee—

'Gio?'

He eased his fragile and protesting foot out of the car with his one good hand, and then swung round and stood up, propping himself on the door for a moment.

'OK?'

'Bit light-headed.'

She clicked her tongue and took his good arm, draping it round her shoulders and sliding her arm around his waist so she could help him to the door. He didn't lean much weight on her. He couldn't, she was tiny, so he wasn't sure how much of a help it was, but it gave him a legitimate excuse to be close to her for a moment.

He actually didn't need her help. So long as he took

tiny, short steps, it was OK. Not good, but OK. And if he took it slowly, he'd be fine.

Did he tell her that?

No, because he was weak and self-indulgent, and he was enjoying the feel of her arm around his waist too much, so he told himself he didn't want to hurt her feelings.

As if it would. Anita was made of sterner stuff than that. He'd ripped her head off a million times when she'd been helping him limp home after he'd fallen out of a tree or off a wall or come hurtling off his bike at some crazy break-neck speed, and she'd never once turned a hair or paid any attention to his objections.

So he kept quiet and let her help him, and enjoyed the side-effect of being close to her firm, athletic body, savouring the nudge of her hip against his, the feel of her arm around his back, her warm fingers curled around his wrist.

And the scent of her, the perfume she always wore, the perfume he'd bought her countless times for Christmas or birthdays, always apologising for being unimaginative but doing it anyway because that scent, for him, was Anita.

'All right now?'

He nodded, words failing him for a second, and she shot him a keen look.

'You really are feeling rough, aren't you? I was expecting you to tell me to let go and stop interfering and that you didn't need my help and go and do something useful like cooking—'

She broke off, meeting his eyes and then laughing as she saw the wry humour reflected there.

'Surely not? Surely you haven't finally learned to be gracious, Giovanni Valtieri, after all these years?'

'Hardly.'

He chuckled and lifted his good hand, patting her cheek

patronisingly. It always annoyed her and her eyes flared in warning.

'Don't push your luck,' she said, and dropping him there in the entrance hall like a hot brick, she stalked into the kitchen, hips swishing. 'Coffee?'

He followed her slowly, enjoying the view in a masochistic way because there was no way he would act on this crazy attraction between them. 'Only if you've got a decent coffeemaker now. I don't suppose there's any food in the house?'

'Not yet. It's in the car. I'll put the coffee on. Do you want to lie down for a while, or sit in here?'

And there it was—the sofa, an old battered leather one where he'd nearly lost his self-control last June. But it looked really inviting, and it was set opposite a pair of French doors out onto the terrace and he could see the familiar lights of the valley twinkling in the distance. His home was out there somewhere in the darkness, and if he couldn't be there, then this was the next best thing.

'Here looks good,' he said, and made his way over to it and lowered himself down cautiously. So far, so good, he thought, and stretched his leg out in front of him with a quiet groan of relief.

'Better?'

'Much better. Have you got that coffee on yet?'

'I thought you didn't like my coffee?'

'I don't, but I need caffeine, and it has to be better than the stuff in the hospital.'

She gave him a look, but got two mugs out and found some biscuits in a tin.

'Here. Eat these while you wait. We'll be having dinner in a while. I bought something ready-made so we can have it whenever you're ready.'

'Good. I'm starving.'

She laughed. 'I've never known you when you weren't starving. It's a miracle you're not fat.'

'It's my enormous brain. It takes a lot of energy.'

She snorted, but he could see a smile teasing the corners of her mouth, and he turned away so she wouldn't see him laughing in response. Then his smile faded, and he closed his eyes and sighed quietly.

If it wasn't for this intense physical tug between them which had appeared suddenly when they were fourteen and never faded, life would have been so, so much easier. They could have just been friends, just as they had all their lives until that point. They'd been inseparable, getting into all manner of scrapes together, but then their hormones had made things awkward between them and she'd started spending more time with the girls, and he with the boys.

But despite the occasional awkwardness, they'd stayed friends, and they still were, twenty years later. She was the first person he called if he had something interesting or sad or exciting to share, but since that time five years ago when they'd somehow lost their restraint and ended up in bed for a few giddy and delirious weeks, things hadn't been the same.

He hadn't called her as much, hadn't leant on her in the same way, and if she'd leant on him, he'd given only what he'd had to and no more.

He'd been easing away from her, trying to distance himself because it was just too darned hard to be so close when he could never give her what she wanted—until last June, when he'd nearly lost the plot. He'd hardly seen anything of her since then, and he'd missed her more than he would ever admit.

* * *

She heard a quiet sigh, and looked over to where he was sitting.

He looked thoughtful, sombre, and she wondered what he was thinking about. The silly woman who'd got him in this mess with her unprovoked attack?

Or the last time he'd sat on that sofa, when they'd so nearly—

'Here, your coffee,' she said, dumping it down on the table beside him. She went back for her own coffee and the biscuits, and handed them to him.

'No chocolate ones?'

'Do you know, you're like a demanding child,' she grumbled, going back to the cupboard and rummaging around until she found a packet of chocolate coated wafers. 'Here. I was saving them for a special occasion, but since you can't cope without them...'

He arched a brow, but she ignored it and tore the Cellophane and put the packet down on the cushions between them, reaching for one at the same time as him. Their fingers clashed, and she withdrew her hand.

'After you,' she said, 'since you're clearly going to die if you don't eat soon,' and his mouth curved into a slight, fleeting smile and he picked one up deliberately and bit it in half.

She looked away. He was teasing her, tormenting her, but her fingers were still tingling from the brush of his hand.

How could she feel like this still? Always, all the time, year after year without anything but hope to feed it?

Except he'd given her hope. They'd had an affair, and last year, they'd so nearly started it up again. So very, very nearly—

'Good biscuits.'

'They are. That's why I was saving them. Don't eat them all, you won't want your dinner.'

'Unlikely.'

She snorted, and put the rest away in the tin and put the lid on, and he just leant back and stretched out his long, rangy body and sighed.

He looked so good there, as if the sofa was made for him, as if it was his body that had moulded it to the saggy, comfortable shape it now was—except he'd only ever been on it once before, and she really, really didn't want to think about that time.

'How's the coffee?' she asked to distract herself, and he glanced down into the mug and shrugged.

'It's coffee. It's not great. Why don't we go and buy a coffee maker?'

'Now?'

He chuckled wearily. 'No, not now. Tomorrow? I don't know if I can cope for two weeks without proper coffee.'

'This is proper coffee. You're just a coffee snob.'

'No, I just know what I like.'

'And you couldn't possibly compromise to spare my feelings?'

He turned his head and gave her a mocking smile. 'Now, you know that's ridiculous.'

Oh, goodness, she couldn't do this! That smile cut right through her defences and left her so vulnerable to him, but there was no way he was going to know that. So she laughed and hit him lightly with a cushion, then hugged it to her chest and pulled her knees up, propping her feet on the edge of the sofa and changing the subject back to the safer one of his attacker.

'I wonder when they'll find her. She makes me nervous.'

His lips kinked in that lopsided smile that was so familiar to her and made her heart lurch once again. 'It's not a Bond movie, Anita. She's just an angry woman who's probably now very scared.'

She nodded. 'Probably. What on earth did she want from you?'

He shrugged. 'Money? They were in business, she cheated him for years, he found out and told her to go quietly and broke up the partnership, and then she decided to go after what she thought was her half. So he produced all the evidence to show she'd cheated him and she gave in, but instead of gaining money, she's ended up with a legal bill, and she blames me.'

Anita laughed in astonishment. 'Why? She didn't seriously expect to win?'

'Apparently.'

'She's deluded, then. Either that or she hasn't heard of your reputation. She should have just gone quietly.'

'Of course, but she was distraught. Much more so than I would have expected, and she was so insistent on talking to me. It wasn't normal behaviour. Maybe if I'd listened I wouldn't be in this mess now.'

He looked slightly bemused, as if he was still trying to work it out, and she reached out a hand and rested it on his shoulder. Silly of her to touch him, so risky and not really necessary, but she needed to feel his warmth, just to reassure herself that he *was* still alive, that this woman's actions hadn't actually caused his death after all.

But then he turned his head and their eyes locked. His pupils flared, darkening his already dark eyes to midnight, and it was as if all the air had been sucked out of the room. Heat scorched through her, a heat born of want and need and a deep and unbearable longing to just lean over and rest her head on his shoulder and hold him close.

For an age they said nothing, and then she pulled her hand away and got up.

'I'll get the food in from the car and cook the dinner,' she said, her voice jerky and tight, and pulling her boots back on, she went out to the car and stood for a moment sucking in the cool air and getting herself back under control.

How could she still love him, still want him, like this? Five years she'd had to get over him, and she'd thought she was doing OK, but tonight she felt as if she hadn't made any progress at all. And now they were supposed to be stuck together alone here for two weeks, and keep their hands to themselves?

They'd never do it.

He was on the phone when she went back inside with the shopping, talking to his mother.

She could tell it was her, just by the tone of his voice and the patient, slightly indulgent expression on his face.

'I'll be fine. Don't worry about me, Anita's looking after me. Of course I'll be nice to her. I know she's a nice girl.' He glanced across at her and winked, and then his mother said something else and he looked hastily away. 'Don't be silly. Of course not.'

Of course not what? Of course not, any chance of them getting back together? It would make his mother a very happy woman. Hers also. Her, too, come to that, happiest of all of them, but it was a fruitless waste of energy thinking about it any more, so she dumped the shopping down on the worktop and started to put it away.

If only she could tune out the sound of his voice, instead of catching every word as if she was eavesdropping! Not that she could help it.

She left the shopping and went into the bathroom, giving it a quick clean. Hopefully by the time she'd finished, he would have got off the phone and she wouldn't be forced to endure the warm murmur of his voice and that soft chuckle which melted her bones.

By the time the taps and mirror were gleaming and they could have eaten off the fittings, she decided the bathroom was probably clean enough. She went back into the kitchen, but he was still on the phone. To Luca, this time, she thought.

There was medical stuff—details of his treatment, a report on what hurt, what tingled, what ached—definitely Luca. And he was lying, as well. She took the phone from him.

'Luca? Hi. This is mostly lies. He hurts, he looks awful, he's dizzy—Gio, no, you can't have the phone back.' She stepped further away, listening to Luca's advice for feeding him things to replace the iron while Gio protested from the confines of the sofa.

'Will do.'

'And don't let him walk on that foot yet.'

'OK. I'll do my best.' She swatted his hand away. 'He wants you back.'

'Anita, before you go, I know this is difficult for you,' Luca said softly. 'We're really grateful to you for being there for him. You just take care, OK? Don't let yourself get hurt, and if it all gets too much, call, and one of us will come.'

She swallowed hard. 'I'm fine. Here he is.'

She handed the phone back and retreated to the kitchen, wishing she'd bought raw ingredients instead of a ready-made meal. It might have given her something to do for the next hour or so, instead of turning on the oven, putting the pan of lasagne into it and then twiddling her thumbs for half an hour.

She closed the oven door and thought about what Luca had said. Dark green vegetables and red meat, with whole grain bread and pulses.

Well, the red meat was taken care of, and she had some pâté and a mixed salad she could give him for a starter, and the ciabatta was made with stoneground flour. That would have to do for now, and tomorrow she'd go shopping.

She pulled plates out and started arranging the salad. He was watching the television now, flicking through the channels, and then he stopped. 'Oh, no, for heaven's sake, why can't they leave me alone?'

'What?'

'It's made the news. Look. The police said it might and they were going to do some damage limitation, but it doesn't sound like it.'

She put the knife down and went over, perching on the end of the sofa and watching.

'Police say Giovanni Valtieri was released from hospital at midday today following an incident yesterday in which he was assaulted. He was seen being driven away from the hospital by a woman believed to be Anita Della Rosso, a friend of the family and one-time girlfriend of the lawyer, who's been at his side since the incident.'

'What!' She plonked down onto the sofa next to him and stared at the television in astonishment. 'How did they find that out?'

He shrugged. 'They're everywhere. Listen.'

There was a reporter standing outside the hospital now, talking about how she'd been seen arriving yesterday and again this morning, and then further talk about their relationship.

'A hugely successful lawyer in his own right, Giovanni is the colourful and flamboyant youngest son of Vittorio and Elisa Valtieri, members of one of Tuscany's oldest and most respected families, and his renewed relationship with society wedding planner Anita Della Rossa is bound to be a cause for speculation. Will Anita be planning her own wedding soon?'

The screen went suddenly blank, and she looked at Gio.

His face was rigid, his lips pressed tightly together into a straight line, a muscle in his jaw jumping. He threw down the remote control and sat back, arms folded, fulminating in silence.

He was furious, she could tell, but more than that, he was worried.

He dragged in a breath and turned to her.

'I never should have dragged you into this. All this talk about our relationship—it's so public, and now they're going to point Camilla Ponti straight at you.'

She smiled a little ruefully and touched his cheek. 'Gio, it's OK. This is my private bolt-hole, a secret hideout that hardly anybody knows about. She won't look for us here, everyone thinks I live either in my apartment in Firenze or with my parents. There's nothing to link it to me, not even the address. I give my parents' villa as my postal address here. This is just like a guest villa.'

'Talking of your parents, you'd better warn them,' he said. 'If they're watching this news bulletin—'

Her phone rang, right on cue, and she spent the next five minutes telling her mother he was all right, they were at her villa and it was all just idle speculation. She was simply looking after an old friend.

'You expect me to believe that? There's no smoke without fire, Anita.'

She coloured. Her mother didn't know about their brief affair five years ago. Nobody did, not really. They certainly hadn't told anyone. Luca and Massimo had guessed, but nobody else had, as far as she knew. Well, apart from the press and now half of Tuscany—

'It's just rumour,' she said lightly. 'Ignore it. I have to go, I'm cooking supper for us.'

But her mother wasn't stupid. 'Take care, *carissima*,' she said softly, and Anita swallowed.

'I will. *Ciao*, Mamma. Love to Papà.'

She lowered her phone and met his eyes.

'Is she OK?'

'She's fussing.'

'Of course she's fussing, she's your mother. I'm surprised she's not over here right now checking the sleeping arrangements.'

'Well, she'll be disappointed, then, because I've made up the spare room for you. Do you want to eat where you are, or at the table?'

'Here? Do you mind? I can't be bothered to move.'

Subtext: it'll hurt too much, even though he'd had his painkillers with coffee earlier. She took his food over to him, with a glass of wine to wash it down.

Not that she approved, but it might help relax him and she wasn't in the mood to play his mother.

'Thanks, that looks really good. I can't tell you how hungry I am.'

She'd spread the pâté on the toasted ciabatta, so he could eat it one-handed, and he forked in the salad and mopped up the dressing with the last of the toast. 'That was good. Tasty. What can I smell?'

'Lasagne. I thought you could eat it with a fork.'

'Great idea.'

She took his plate and brought it back with the lasagne on it, and after they'd eaten it he leant back and sighed in contentment.

'Better?'

'Amazing. That was really good. I was ready for it. I haven't eaten anything proper since the day before yesterday.'

He rolled his head towards her, his eyes serious, the food forgotten. 'Anita, I hate involving you in this. You should be on holiday, not sitting here babysitting me while they gossip about us on the news.'

'Don't worry. I don't care if people talk about us.'

'Well, I do, and I'm not thrilled about them giving Camilla Ponti directions.'

'She won't come after you,' she said with more confidence than she felt. 'She's in Firenze somewhere, trying to hide from the police. Even she's going to realise she's in deep enough trouble without making it worse. And anyway, I thought you said she was mortified.'

'She was. She really didn't mean to hurt me.'

'Well, then, we'll be fine,' she said firmly. 'The outside lights come on if anyone approaches, so we can't be sneaked up on. I'll set the alarm and put the car in the garage, and nobody would know we were here, if that makes you happier.'

What would make him happier was knowing that Camilla Ponti had been found and seen by a doctor. Until then, this would have to do.

'Fine.'

'Good. Now I think it's time you went to bed.'

Their eyes clashed again, and then he levered himself to his feet.

'You'd better show me to my room, then,' he said, and

she led him down the hall and pushed open the bedroom door. She'd unpacked his bag and laid his things out on the top of the chest, including his painkillers.

He was pleased to see them. He'd just had some, but he had no doubt he'd need more before the night was out. He hobbled awkwardly past her, looked around and then met her eyes again. 'It's a nice room. Thank you.'

'*Prego.* I'll bring you a glass of water. The bathroom's across the hall, and I've put out clean towels and your pills are on the chest. Will you be all right getting ready for bed, or do you want me to help you undress?'

He gave a soft huff of laughter.

'I don't think that's a good idea.'

Their eyes locked, his dark and unfathomable. As well as she knew him, she couldn't read them.

She could feel the heat scorching her cheeks, but she held her ground. 'I thought you weren't feeling great.'

'I'm not, but I'd have to be dead before I let you undress me. *Buonanotte,* Anita.'

And he closed the door softly in her face.

CHAPTER THREE

He stood there for a moment, listening, and after a long pause he heard the sound of her banging around in the kitchen.

She sounded mad with him. Not surprising, really. It hadn't been the politest rejection, and she'd only been trying to help, but—*Dio,* just being that close to her was killing him, and he might not be feeling great today, but his body clearly didn't care about that. It was interested in Anita, and saying so.

No *way* was she taking off his clothes and finding that out!

Which meant he had to do it on his own, and frankly he wasn't sure he could one-handed. The first thing he had to do, though, was use the bathroom, because he wasn't going to wander around the house half naked. He knew his limitations, and keeping a lid on his libido was one of them. The more he was wearing when he was exposed to her, frankly, the better.

There was no sign of his washbag, so he assumed she must have put it in the bathroom already. He frowned, feeling another pang of guilt, which was silly. It was nothing he wouldn't have done for her, and he wouldn't have taken no for an answer about helping her undress, either.

Clearly his skin was tougher than hers. And she wouldn't have been so rude.

Guilt again.

He limped to the bathroom, spent a few infuriating minutes in there struggling to clean his teeth with the wrong hand, and when he opened the door she was outside.

She hadn't been able to stay away. She'd gone into the kitchen, steaming mad with him, deeply hurt—

I'd have to be dead before I let you undress me.

What was that about? He'd been keen enough for her to undress him five years ago, for goodness' sake, so what on earth had changed so much that he wouldn't even let her help him when he was injured? She'd thought they were friends still, but clearly not. They'd crossed a line when they'd had the affair, and now—now everything was different, and there was no going back.

They couldn't just undo the fact that they'd been lovers. She realised that, but this was nothing to *do* with sex! Except clearly, for him, taking off his clothes was something he did on his own, or a prelude to lovemaking. Often, for them, the only prelude, she remembered, because on occasions they'd been so desperate they'd almost torn each other's clothes off—

'Oh, stop it! This is ridiculous!'

She slammed the dishwasher shut, battened down the hatches on her memories and swiped a cloth over the worktop. The plates were in the dishwasher, the kitchen was tidy.

And still he was in the bathroom.

In difficulties?

So she'd gone to investigate, listened outside to the sounds of frustration as he struggled with something— his toothbrush?

And then the door opened, and she saw the pain etched into his face, the frustration, the tiredness, and she just wanted to hug him. He shook his head, closing his eyes briefly, and when he opened them she could see guilt written all over his face.

Goodness knows what was written on hers. It must be a mass of emotions, and it seemed he could read them all.

'I'm sorry, *cara*,' he said gruffly, reaching out one-handed to hug her, and then she was there against him, her arms around him, her face buried in his chest just breathing him in and holding on.

'I'm sorry I flounced off,' she mumbled. 'You look awful. I've been so worried about you—'

Her voice hitched, and he sighed and rubbed her back gently. 'I'm fine, Anita. Come on, don't cry. Go and make us some hot chocolate, and I'll get my clothes off. No more tears, eh?'

She eased away, sniffing slightly and scrubbing tears from her cheeks. 'Sorry. I'm such an idiot—'

'You're a lovely idiot. I'm lucky to have such a good friend.'

There. He'd said it. Friend.

Not lover.

She nodded, and walked away towards the kitchen to make the hot chocolate, and he gritted his teeth and made it the last few steps to the bedroom.

Then he looked at his foot.

The nurses had struggled to get his trousers on over it without hurting him. What hope did he have, one-handed? He couldn't do it alone.

Which meant asking Anita.

She came back with the hot chocolate while he was sitting on the side of the bed scowling.

'Problem?'

'I can't get my trousers off on my own,' he said grudgingly.

She suppressed a smile. 'No, I don't suppose you can. And you need something to keep the weight off your foot in the night.' She plonked the chocolate down on the bedside table, threw the bottom of the quilt back and put two pillows in the bed.

'OK. That should do it. So, are you sleeping in the trousers, bearing in mind that you'd have to be dead to let me help you?'

He winced at the mild tone which belied a world of hurt—hurt of his making. He deserved her sarcasm. Hell, he deserved more than that. It would serve him right if she left him to struggle on his own. So he swallowed his pride. He needed her help, like it or not, and he realised he might have to grovel to get it.

'I'm sorry. I didn't mean that quite as it came out. No, I'm not sleeping in them, but I have no idea how to get them off, I just know it's going to hurt.'

'Not if I do it—assuming you'll let me help you?' she asked more gently.

He shrugged, hating it but out of options, and unfastened his trousers, pushing them down to his knees before sitting back down on the edge of the bed. He felt naked and vulnerable. Ridiculous. He'd been fine with the nurses, so why was he worried about Anita?

Because I know what it's like to make love to her.

'Just do it, Anita,' he said, and she gave a little shrug and knelt down at his feet, which brought her eyes in line with the telltale bulge in his jersey shorts. And just south, on the inside of his muscular thigh, was the transparent dressing over his wound.

She winced. 'That was close. It could have been really catastrophic.'

'My sex life's not really your problem,' he said shortly, struggling with her proximity and wishing she'd just look somewhere else before he gave himself away, but she just rolled her eyes.

'I wasn't thinking about your sex life,' she bit back drily. 'But since you mention it, there are all those children you might never have been able to have. That would be a waste.'

'Except I'm not planning on having any children, *cara*. No way. I'm not cut out to be a father.'

She sat back on her heels and stared up at him, astonished. 'What? That's ridiculous, you'd be a marvellous father,' she said crossly. 'You're wonderful with your brothers' children. They adore you.'

He shrugged. 'So? I'm their uncle, I spoil them. It changes nothing. I'm not having children, ever. I don't want the responsibility. If I did, I would have done something about it.'

With her? Hardly. The moment their relationship had started to look cosy and semi-permanent, he'd legged it into the wide blue yonder. But one day, surely, with someone…?

'You might change your mind,' she said doggedly. 'It would be a shame to waste all the potential in those genes.'

'Potential for what?' he asked, exasperated. 'I've told you, I've got no intention of passing on my genes to anyone. There isn't a woman in the world who could talk me into it.'

Well, that was telling her, she thought, and under the resignation—because after all, she knew her relationship with him was going nowhere—was a pang of what felt like grief. She'd dreamed of it so many times, could conjure up an image of a child with his eyes and her hair, but only if she let herself, and she didn't, because she didn't want to lose what was left of her sanity. He'd had quite enough of that already.

'Well, that's a shame,' she said lightly, trying to make a joke out of it. 'I mean, I don't want to inflate your ego, but you're healthy, passably good-looking and when you aren't tripping over your own refuse bag, you're reasonably intelligent. You could have some quite nice children, so long as they didn't inherit your attitude.'

It was the sort of sassy remark he expected from her, so without thinking he came straight back at her.

'*Dio*, you can talk! What about your attitude?'

'There's no chance your children will inherit my attitude, is there? You made that quite clear five years ago.'

There was a second of shocked silence, and then he reached out a hand and touched her cheek.

'Anita?'

To his astonishment she blushed and turned her head away. 'Ignore me,' she mumbled. 'I'm just worried about you.'

He frowned. 'Well, you don't need to be.' He sighed and rammed his hand through his hair, then winced. He'd have to remember to use the other one, but right now he was so tired and sore he was ready to fall over, and her words had created a sudden, shocking image of a cheeky little girl with a sassy smile and a wit like a razor. And it took the wind right out of his sails.'I need to get to bed,' he said abruptly.

'Sorry,' she muttered, and then she hooked off his left boot and eased the trousers down, first off his left foot, then very carefully over his right. Then she peeled the sock off.

He flexed his ankle slightly and winced as she sat back on her heels and looked at it.

'It's an impressive colour,' she said, getting to her feet.

He peered at it thoughtfully. It was black and blue, the bits he could see of it around the strapping, and no doubt in time it would go all shades of the rainbow. He looked forward to it. It might hurt less by then.

He eased back onto the mattress, unable to use his bad hand to shift himself, refusing to ask her help, but she gave it anyway, hooking her arm in his armpit and hauling the bad side up the bed while he shoved the good side.

Then she plumped the pillows and covered him carefully with the quilt, hesitating to frown down at his thigh.

'Is it all right? Does the dressing need changing?'

'No. They've given me a supply of fresh dressings, but they'd told me to leave it for a day or so. It should be fine— assuming I can peel it off the hairs.'

Her laugh had a little mocking edge to it that he didn't like. 'It'll be like having a leg wax. I'm sure you'll cope, you big baby.'

He winced, and she laughed again, then her smile faded and she reached out a cool, gentle hand and laid it on his leg, just below the wound, all signs of mockery gone.

'Even if it is none of my business, I'm glad the glass hasn't done any lasting damage,' she said a little gruffly as she covered him up and gave him back some privacy.

'As you were kind enough to point out, if I hadn't been so stupid we wouldn't be sitting here having this conversation.' He patted the bedcovers beside him. 'Come here. Grab the hot chocolate and turn out the light, and come and sit with me for a bit. I'm too tired to argue with you.'

'That'll be a first,' she said drily, but she climbed up onto the bed beside him, wriggling back against the pillows and handing him his hot chocolate before turning off the bedside light so they could see the twinkling lights in the distance. For a moment he said nothing, then he gave a contented sigh.

'I love that view,' he said quietly. 'Utter blackness, with just the faintest glimmer from the villages. It's never as dark in the city, and I really miss it.'

'I do, too. The view's the main reason I wanted to renovate this villa. Sometimes I sit here at night and stare at it for hours,' she said. 'It seems odd without lights on at the *palazzo,* though. I can usually see it from all the main rooms. It's like a beacon.'

'So is that why you look out? To see if I'm there?' he teased.

Ouch. Too close to the truth for comfort, she thought, hoping she wasn't blushing. Once in an evening was enough, but at least it was too dark to see.

'In your dreams,' she said lightly. And hers, but she wasn't giving him that bit of ammunition under any circumstances!

'Have you had your painkillers and antibiotics?' she asked instead, watching him carefully in the dim light from the hall.

He nodded. 'Yes. Anita, I'm fine, really, stop fretting.'

'I can't help it. I can't believe I didn't answer your calls—'

She broke off, not wanting to broach the subject yet again, but he gave a soft huff of laughter.

'Forget it. I'm fine. It was my own stupid fault I was hurt.'

Anita shuddered. 'Not entirely. If she hadn't been there it would never have happened.'

Even in the darkness, she could see him frown, serious at last. 'I know. And I'm concerned that she's still out there. Will you do me a favour? Stay here next to me tonight?'

'What, to protect you?' she teased, but he gave a wry chuckle.

'Hardly. I was thinking more the other way round.'

'You're going to protect me?' Now it was her turn to laugh. 'Gio, you can hardly move!'

'I can stand between you,' he said quietly, and she realised he was deadly serious. His macho nonsense touched her, but the irony of it was so ridiculous she didn't know whether to laugh or cry.

'Gio, she won't come here.'

'You don't know that. If it hadn't been on the news, I wouldn't have worried, but as it has…'

His voice trailed off, and she gave in.

He wanted to protect her, and for the sake of his peace of mind, she'd let him think he was, but there was no danger from Camilla Ponti that she could see. The only danger to her in this villa was Gio himself, and she wasn't strong enough to resist him.

But she knew him well enough to know that she wouldn't win the argument, so she did the next best thing. She agreed.

'All right. If you insist. I'll get ready for bed and come back.'

'Don't forget to lock up.'

She rolled her eyes. 'Well, isn't it just as well I've got you here to remind me of something so obvious.'

It actually suited her to be beside him, because she

wanted to keep an eye on him and make sure he was all right. She just had to resist the urge to fall into his arms.

Not that there'd be much to resist. He was exhausted and injured, and if nothing else the pills would make him sleep.

And as long as he was this sick and this sore, she'd be safe.

Ish.

'Give me five minutes,' she said, and retreated.

It was OK to start with.

She was wearing pyjamas—not little bits of fluff, but real pyjamas with a long-sleeved top and trousers. She just felt safer that way—safer from herself, but she needn't have worried, because he stayed firmly on his side, and she stayed firmly on hers.

Until she woke in the night to hear him muttering and thrashing around, and she reached out her hand and rested in on his chest.

'Gio! Gio, wake up, you're dreaming!'

He grunted, and she felt the tension drain out of him with a whoosh.

'Sorry—I didn't mean to disturb you.'

'It's fine. Are you OK?'

'I am now. Come here.'

And he reached out his left arm and scooped her into his good side. She laid her head against his chest, listening to the drumming of his heart, and gradually it slowed to a steady, even beat.

She rested her hand over it and wondered what he'd been dreaming about. The attack? Probably, she thought, with another stab of guilt for not answering her phone. She tried not to think how different it might have been if the ambulance hadn't got there in time, if the woman hadn't called for help.

Very different.

She might have been visiting him in the hospital mortuary instead of lying here beside him, and the thought brought with it a wave of emotion that made her catch her breath.

Losing him because he didn't want her was one thing. Losing him because he'd been killed in a stupid accident was another altogether. She'd been without him for all of her adult life, except for a few short, blissful weeks, but she'd always known he was still walking around in the world, still out there with that razor-sharp intellect and the tongue to go with it, and just knowing that somehow made it all bearable.

To lose him to death, never to hear his voice again or see his face, never to be near him again, just didn't bear thinking about.

So she snuggled closer, resting her legs against his left one, her toes nudging his foot. Just in contact, nothing more.

Until the next time she woke, to find she'd shifted, draped her leg over his, so that his firm, hard thigh was between hers, the pressure making her ache for him in a way she'd forgotten.

No. Not forgotten. Put out of her mind, but not any more. Now, it was right back there in the forefront, and she shifted against him, trying to ease the ache.

He moved his leg, lifting it slightly towards her, and she made a tiny, needy noise.

This was crazy! He was injured, there was no way this was going anywhere, and she ought to move out of his arms and—

'Where are you going?'

'I'm lying on you. I'm afraid I'll hurt you.'

'You're not hurting me, you're fine. Stay there.' His arm tightened and pulled her closer.

She slept again, but her body was far from relaxed, and she woke again some time later from a lurid dream to the building, driving sensation of a climax on the brink.

Still half asleep and in the clutches of the dream, she bit her lip as she felt the sensation explode through her body, the shockwave stealing her breath so she could only gasp his name.

'Anita?' He turned his head, feeling the tremors running through her, the clench of her thighs against his, and need rocketed through him.

Her beautiful body was convulsing against him, his name a broken whisper on her lips. He tilted her head, his mouth finding hers and plundering it, swallowing the gasps and sighs still coming from her body as the shockwave died away. *Dio*, he wanted her. Crazily, improbably, he wanted her, wanted to bury himself deep inside her and drive into her again and again—

'Ahh!'

He dropped his right leg back to the mattress, letting the tension out of the protesting thigh muscle, feeling the nudge of the pillows against his ankle. Damn.

She lifted her head. 'Gio?'

'It's OK,' he said, ignoring the pain, running his hand over her back and soothing her. He still wanted her, despite the pain, and his mouth found hers again in the darkness, frustration killing him.

'I can't,' he groaned. 'I need you, I want you so much, but I just can't.' He swore softly, rocking against her leg, grunting with pain as his thigh tightened again.

And then she slid her hand slowly, hesitantly over his chest, down past his ribs, tightening the muscles of his abdomen as she glided over them and under the waistband of his shorts. He thought he'd die as her fingers circled him, her delicate grip torture. Then she tightened her hand, moved it slowly in firm, even strokes, and he felt the pressure mounting relentlessly.

He dropped his head back, lifted his hips and let out a long, shuddering groan as she took him over the edge and everything crashed and burned around him.

And then reality hit, like a bucket of cold water, as the pain penetrated his emerging consciousness and common sense returned.

What the *hell* was he doing? With Anita, of all people? He'd ended it five years ago, tried to stay away from her, for her sake, because he couldn't be relied on, couldn't be trusted in a relationship, could never seem to give enough to make a woman truly happy. He'd done it so she could move on with her life, find another man, settle down, have the babies she so clearly wanted. And it was working, sort of. She was dating from time to time. She'd get there, if he could only leave her alone.

But he couldn't, apparently. And now, here, when he needed her for so many other reasons, he'd gone and blown it by doing this.

He hadn't needed her by his side all night. He'd *wanted* her by his side. It was nothing to do with the Ponti woman, because he truly didn't think she'd hurt them. It was all to do with wanting Anita.

It was *always* to do with wanting Anita.

'Gio? Are you OK?'

Her voice was soft, her hand stroking his chest now,

the touch tender, as if he was a child—or maybe just an injured lover.

He wasn't her lover. He couldn't be her lover.

'Why did you do that?' he asked harshly, his voice not quite as steady as he would have liked.

There was a tiny gasp, and she pulled her hand away from his chest as if it was red hot, eased her body away from his, and he felt cold air move in to fill the space where she had been. It made his heart ache.

'I'm sorry,' she mumbled. 'I thought—'

'Forget it. I need the bathroom.'

He got out of bed and limped painfully across the hall. Hell, his foot hurt, but there was no way he was asking her to help him. Not after that.

It had been too darned personal, but it wasn't enough. He wanted to get a lot, lot more personal, starting right now.

He stood in front of the bathroom mirror for ages, staring at himself in disgust. He was still hard. He still wanted her. Even after—

He willed his body to co-operate. It took an age, and when he finally went back to bed she'd gone, her bedroom door firmly closed.

Probably just as well, he thought guiltily, easing himself back under the covers, but it was cold and lonely without her, and he cursed himself for ruining it, for kissing her, for reaching out for her. He should have just lain there and pretended to be asleep, but he'd wanted her to touch him.

Well, she had, and now it was going to be thoroughly awkward and difficult between them, and he only had himself to blame.

She didn't sleep again that night.

Instead, she lay in her bed, feeling cold and lonely and

embarrassed. How could she have been so stupid? So ridiculously uninhibited?

She gave a tiny howl of frustration and turned her face into the pillow. It was going to be so difficult now between them. It had been hard enough before. Now it would be impossible. It was going to be utterly humiliating facing him in the morning, even though it hadn't really been her fault. How could she control her body in its sleep?

But she hadn't been asleep, she reminded herself bluntly. Not for all of it. Not when she'd touched him. Not when she'd kissed him back, and slid her hand down into his shorts and wrapped the hot, silky length of him in her palm—

'No!'

She stifled the tiny scream of frustration and humiliation, and pulled the quilt up over her head. Stupid, stupid, stupid. How was she supposed to face him after that? She might not get up again.

Ever.

His phone rang at seven thirty—not too early under normal circumstances, but after the unscheduled scene in the night he'd only just dropped off to sleep again and for a second he considered not answering it.

He was glad he did.

It was the police, to tell him that Camilla Ponti had walked into the police station in Firenze in a distraught state, saying she'd nearly killed him.

'She didn't hurt me. It was an accident, but I do think she needs to see a doctor, because she wasn't rational. Do you need me to come and talk to her?' he asked, but the detective told him it was unnecessary.

'You just concentrate on getting better, and leave her to us. We'll take care of her.'

'Good. Call me if you need anything.'

He put the phone down, blew his breath out and lay back on the pillows.

They'd got her.

Which meant, of course, that there was less justification for him to stay here hiding out with Anita.

He waited for the feeling of relief, but it didn't come. Instead, he just felt a little flat. Ridiculous. He'd go back to Firenze and pick up his life where he'd left off. Maybe even go on holiday with his family after all.

Except that it was a skiing holiday and anyway, Anita was supposed to be there, too.

Oh, hell. It was all too complicated, and a more immediate concern was having a shower. How, he had no idea, but the first step was getting to the bathroom.

He threw back the covers and eased himself to the edge of the bed. He was still sitting there psyching himself up for the walk when there was a tap at the open door and she came in, wrapped in a bath robe with her hair in a towel, obviously fresh from the shower.

She smelt amazing, and he groaned inwardly as she walked over to him and leant on the end of the bed, her hands fiddling with the belt of her robe.

'Who was that on the phone?'

'The police. They've got her. She turned herself in. Apparently she's in a hell of a state.'

'Oh. Right.'

She looked down into his face, and he could see just how awkward she felt this morning. Just as awkward as him.

'About last night—'

They both broke off, and his mouth twitched into a smile and he raised a brow, gesturing with his head for her to continue.

'I'm sorry. I overstepped the mark. I didn't mean to, I was half asleep and I don't really know what happened. It won't happen again.'

He felt curiously disappointed, and nearly laughed at himself. 'Forget it. As you say, you were asleep. I kissed you, I pushed it, encouraged you—hell, I begged you, Anita, and I had no right to be so harsh with you. I'm the one who should be sorry.'

He wasn't, though, he realised. Not really. And given the choice, he'd do it all over again. So he couldn't give himself the choice.

'It won't happen again, anyway, because I'm going back to Firenze,' he announced bluntly, and she stared at him as if he was mad.

'What? Why? How? How will you manage?'

'What do you mean, how will I manage?'

She rolled her eyes and stood back, hands on hips. 'You can't manage one-handed. You can't do any one of a number of things with only one hand! You're going to have to change the dressing on your leg—what are you going to do, ring your neighbour's doorbell and ask them to do it? Don't be silly! And how will you cook?'

'The same way I always do. I'll pick up the phone.'

'And go to the door and let them in. You don't even have a lift in that building. How will you manage the stairs with that ankle?'

She was right. Maddeningly, annoyingly right.

'I'll go and join the rest of the family, then.'

'On a skiing holiday?' she said, looking pointedly at his foot. 'Sounds great.'

'Well, I haven't got a lot of options, have I, really? Carlotta and Roberto are away, so it's my apartment or the ski chalet.'

'Or you could just stay here.'

Her words hung in the air between them, fraught with the memory of last night.

He thought about it. He could stay there, sure, but would it be wise? Probably not. Safe? Unlikely. Appealing?

Oh, yes.

'On one condition,' he said, feeling himself surrender.

'Which is?'

'We go out this morning and buy a coffee maker.'

She stared at him blankly for a second, then she let out a tiny huff of astonished laughter.

'Done. I'm going to get dressed. Do you need any help?'

'No.'

Probably not true, that, but he'd manage if it killed him.

She nodded, and walked towards the door. 'OK. Yell if you need me.'

Need? He'd never stopped needing her, not for a day in the last twenty years. But he was no good for her, and the sooner she found herself a nice, decent, reliable man to make her happy and give her babies—babies without his attitude—the happier he'd be.

He frowned, put the babies firmly out of his mind and headed for the bathroom. A shower could wait. In the meantime, he could wash and dress himself, even if it was agony. He had to regain some independence from Anita if he was going to be able to manage this situation.

He could do this. He could keep his distance, accept her friendship at face value and leave at the end of the fortnight.

He just needed to toughen up.

CHAPTER FOUR

THEY skipped breakfast.

The lure of a rich, dark double espresso was calling him, and Anita knew he'd be grumpy until he had his caffeine shot. Besides, the café they were going to made the most amazing pastries, and she needed comfort food after last night.

She was still squirming with embarrassment every time she thought about it. Well, not just embarrassment, if she was honest. There was a good chunk of lust flung in there, too, and she was beginning to wonder how she'd cope for two weeks until his family came back and took him off her hands.

She must have been mad to suggest it. She should have sent him back to Firenze and let him cope. He could have hired a nurse, for heaven's sake. He had enough money.

'There's a space.'

She turned into the parking bay and cut the engine. They were as close as they could get to the café, and there was a shop almost next door that sold decent bean-to-cup coffee makers. She'd never bought one because she didn't care that much about coffee and they'd always seemed a bit unnecessary, but that was fine. He could have whatever he liked. He was buying.

'I'm ready for this,' he muttered as they arrived at the café, and he pulled out his wallet and ordered his double espresso and her cappuccino. 'What are you eating?'

'Oh, I don't know. I can't decide...'

He ordered a selection before she could vacillate any longer, and while he was paying she found a table by the window and sat down to wait for him.

And wait.

Eventually he came over, a wry smile on his face, and eased himself into the chair with a grunt.

'Sorry. He'd seen the news—wanted to know how I was doing.'

'I'd worked it out, Gio. It's going to happen all the time. You grew up here, of course they're interested.'

'Yeah, he was interested in you, too. Were you planning our wedding yet and that sort of thing.'

Not a chance. Not now, and probably never had been, although she'd let herself believe it for a few delirious weeks.

Move on!

'So, what do you want to do today?' she asked, completely ignoring his last remark because there didn't seem to be anything to say about it, and particularly not in public.

'Apart from buying a coffee maker?' he said drily. 'I don't know. Do you fancy going for a drive? I get cabin fever.'

'That quick?'

He laughed. 'I'm not good when I'm not busy. So, shall we do that? We could drive somewhere and stop for lunch.'

'You haven't even had breakfast yet and you're worrying about the next meal,' she teased. 'Don't worry, I won't let you starve. And sure, we can go for a drive. There's that lovely road high up on the ridge looking towards Monte

Amiata. The views are lovely and we could cut back on the other side along the Val d'Orcia and have lunch in Pienza.'

He nodded, but he didn't look enthused, and Anita began to wonder how she was going to entertain a man who lived life so hard and so fast that he had cabin fever after a day. Less than that. And she had a fortnight to get through?

'I have a better idea.'

Good, she thought, because she had none at all. Well, none that were in any way sensible or wouldn't get her into a whole load of trouble. 'What's that?'

'Let's go back to my apartment and pick up my coffee maker. I've got a spare one—I've got a built-in one now, so it's redundant. You can have it. And I need clothes. All I've got is that overnight bag and it's a bit challenged. I didn't really think it through. And trainers, so I have a shoe I can wear on this foot, and I can bring my laptop. I've got some work I could be doing on a case that's coming up.'

She nodded, relieved that he might actually find something to occupy him, apart from baiting her because they weren't doing what they both wanted to do because he'd decided five years ago that it was off the menu. 'OK.'

She looked up, smiled at the café owner who'd brought over their order and dug into the pastries. She was starving. She hadn't slept at all well last night, and when she had—

Back to that again, she thought, growling silently. Well, at least Camilla Ponti had turned up, so she wouldn't have to spend another night with him so he could 'protect' her. Fat lot of protection. She needed protecting from herself, apparently, as well as him.

'Did I say something to upset you?'

She jerked her head up and met his eyes. 'What? No. Sorry. I was miles away.'

About four miles, to be exact, lying in his bed sprawled all over him and behaving like a hussy. She could feel her cheeks getting hotter, and looked hastily away. 'Good pastries.'

So she was thinking about that, too, he thought, and gave a silent huff of laughter. Oh, well. He'd thought about it for twenty years without acting on it apart from one short and all too memorable month, so he could do it for another fortnight. And if she wanted to talk about food...

'They always are good pastries in here,' he said blandly, biting into one as she looked up.

Their eyes locked, and then her gaze tracked his mouth as he licked his lips. It wasn't deliberate, it wasn't conscious, but her pupils flared as she watched him and he just knew he was in trouble, because last night, entirely by accident, they'd broken all the rules in his little black book.

Starting with rule number one—don't mess with friends. Especially not one you've known since before you could walk. One you've already hurt because you couldn't keep a lid on your lust.

He looked down at the table, located his coffee and took a gulp. It was hot. Too hot, and he felt it burn his tongue, but at least it took his mind off Anita's body.

They arrived in Firenze shortly before lunchtime, and she pulled up next to his Mercedes sports. It was his new toy, and he'd been looking forward to driving it up into the Alps.

And then the Ponti woman—

He cut off that line of thought, got out of the car and saw a shard of broken glass lying on the ground.

He bent and picked it up, and felt a cold shiver run over him.

'Why was she so desperate to talk to me, Anita?' he asked softly, staring at the glass in his hand. 'I was only doing my job. She had no entitlement to that money, and she must have known that. So what was there to say that she so desperately needed me to hear?'

'Who knows? She's a liar and a cheat. Don't waste time thinking about her.'

She all but dragged him towards the door, and he let them in and looked at the stairs.

'Want me to carry you up?' she suggested sassily, and he glowered at her for a second, then gave a reluctant laugh.

'It's very kind of you to offer, but I think I can manage.' He could. Just about. He hopped, he hobbled, and finally they were there and he could sprawl on his sofa and look out over the rooftops to the hills in the distance while he recovered.

'Could you put this glass in the bin? You'd better wrap it. There's a pile of old newspapers in one of the cupboards in the kitchen—and while you're there, I need a coffee.'

Anita, busy taking in the changes he'd made to the kitchen area in the last five years, rolled her eyes. 'You *always* need a coffee. I don't know why I indulge you.' She dealt with the glass, then looked around. 'So, where is it anyway, this new gadget of yours?'

'Under that glass door—no, not that one, that's the steam oven. Next to it. Lift the door up and slide it back.'

She studied it. It seemed pretty straightforward, but some instructions wouldn't go amiss. 'So, how does this thing work?'

'You put beans in it from in the freezer, put a cup under it and press the button. It's not exactly rocket science.'

She ignored the sarcasm. 'Cups? Freezer?'

It would have been easier to get up, but it was more entertaining lying there watching her pottering in his kitchen, so he stayed put and gave her instructions, and every time she bent over to get something out of a cupboard, he was treated to the delectable view of her smooth, rounded bottom in jeans that hugged her lovingly.

His jeans were getting a bit more loving just watching her, and he dragged his eyes away and tried to get himself under control.

Anita threw a glance over her shoulder and saw him flicking idly through a magazine. Sarky swine, she thought. She could have smacked him, but she wouldn't give him the satisfaction. He'd been so different five years ago. He wouldn't have left her alone in the kitchen, he would have been in there, standing behind her with his arms around her, his body warm and hard and very, very close, and sometimes he'd turn her towards him and lift her so she was perched on the edge of the counter, and he'd take her then and there, his eyes hot and smoky with need, and then he'd gather her up in his arms, her legs still locked around his waist, and carry her to the bedroom to finish what he'd started.

Until he ended it, without a word of warning.

'There, was that so hard?' he asked when she set his espresso down in front of him with rather more force than was necessary.

'It's not a case of hard, it's a case of not having seen it before. I'm not an idiot—don't patronise me.'

She was cross, he realised. Cross because she was in his apartment? Cross because he was being an ass? Or cross because the last time she'd been here, he'd been telling her all the reasons why their affair should end?

'I'm sorry,' he said, meaning it. Sorry for all sorts of things. 'Thank you for making the coffee.'

'You don't have to grovel. Have you got anything here to eat?'

'No, not really. I'd run the fridge down because I was going away. There's no milk, either.'

'That's fine. I'll have it black, if it's as good as you say it is. Are you hungry? I could go out and get something.'

'Or we can order pizza.'

He pulled out his phone. It didn't surprise her that the number was on speed-dial, or that the intercom buzzed after just five minutes.

She ran down and paid and carried the steaming box back upstairs and put it on the coffee table in front of him. It was a *quattro stagioni,* with a different topping on each quarter, and she pulled off a slice and ate it hungrily.

'Oh, gorgeous. It's so fresh—where's the pizzeria?'

'Just round the corner. Literally.'

'And they know you well.'

He grinned mischievously. 'Don't tell my mother.'

She studied him, unshaven because it was too challenging to bother with, the stubble on his jaw making him look just a little wicked and slightly dangerous. She felt a shiver of excitement down her spine and crushed it ruthlessly.

'I'm sure of all the things I shouldn't be telling your mother, Giovanni Valtieri, that's the least of them.'

He winked and chuckled, sinking his teeth into the second slice of pizza. The flavour exploded on his tongue, and he sighed contentedly and demolished it, and reached for another, and another.

She left him the last slice, sitting back and wiping her fingers on the paper napkin.

'I can't remember when I last had pizza. That was amazing.'

'It is good there. They use our olives.'

'Do they? I wonder why?' she teased, and he laughed softly.

'Because they're the best?'

'My father might argue, but Massimo would be pleased to hear you say that. He works hard to uphold the family name for quality, and he's very proud of it.'

'And your father?'

She grinned. 'He thinks his olives are better. He concedes on the wine and the cheese.'

'That's because he doesn't make either of them.'

She shrugged, her eyes teasing, and he felt a pang of loss. They'd been so good together, and he'd had real hopes for them, but then reality had intruded with shocking force and reminded him of just what a lousy bet he was.

He couldn't give a relationship what it deserved. He never had, and he was afraid he never could, not even with Anita, and he'd thought it was better for her to get out of it before she got in too deep and ended up destroyed, like Kirsten. And not just Kirsten.

There was enough on his conscience already. Too much. He couldn't have Anita on it as well. Not his dearest friend.

Looking at her now, he felt nothing but regret, but that was selfish. For once, it wasn't all about him and what he wanted, and he knew he was going to have to exercise enormous self-control in the next fortnight. He couldn't let his own selfish wants and needs override his common sense and decency, however much he wanted her. Not if she was ever going to move on and find someone else.

He didn't want to think about that.

'I suppose we should get on,' he said abruptly.

'Probably.' She got to her feet and washed her hands in the sink, then looked around. 'So where's this coffee maker?'

'In that cupboard on the left—no, the next one.'

She opened the cupboard and found it, lifted it out and set it on the worktop. She eyed it dubiously. Apart from the fact that it would take up her entire kitchen, it weighed a ton and she was going to have to carry it downstairs. 'It seems a bit excessive.'

'Where coffee's concerned, nothing is too excessive,' he said emphatically. 'There are some unopened beans in the next cupboard.'

She got them out, put them with the machine and then walked towards his bedroom. She hadn't been in there since their affair, but it hadn't changed a lot.

He had a new blind, but that was it. The bed was the same, she noticed with a pang, swathed in vast acres of the finest threadcount Egyptian cotton; pure white, unadorned, uncomplicated luxury. It was the most comfortable bed she'd ever slept in, and she'd been happier there than she had anywhere in her life.

She'd gone out and bought herself the same bedding after they'd split up, but she hadn't been able to bring herself to use it because just the feel of it reminded her so strongly of him that it broke her heart.

'So, what do you need?' she asked, forcing herself to focus on something other than the bed.

'Underwear, socks, casual shirts, sweaters, trousers—there are some jog bottoms in the bottom drawer in the wardrobe, I think. They might be easier to get on and off over my foot. And my trainers.'

She found them, and the underwear. Soft, clingy jersey shorts that hugged his body enticingly. A heap of socks, all carefully paired. Shirts, hung by colour and style.

'You're a neat freak,' she said drily, throwing the clothes

into a heap ready for packing. He was standing in the doorway, frowning.

'Don't crease those shirts.'

'I thought they were casual? And you're going to be wearing them with jog bottoms.'

'They don't have to look as if I've slept in them.'

She propped herself against the door of the wardrobe and folded her arms.

'Do you want to do this yourself, or would you like me to help you? In which case, you need to shut up.'

He opened his mouth, then clamped it shut in a grim line. She smiled and carried on, and he retrieved a few things from the bathroom, then packed up his laptop and the documents he needed. Ten minutes later they were on their way out.

He limped slowly towards the car with his laptop bag over his shoulder while she made another trip for the coffee maker. By the time she was back with it, he was in the car with his eyes closed.

'Did you bring any painkillers with you?' she asked, and he shook his head.

'I'm fine. Let's just go.'

They went to the supermarket on the way home, to buy things for supper. She'd only done a hasty shop the day before, just enough to tide them over, so she left him in the car and worked her way a bit more systematically along the aisles for something to make that evening.

Nothing too easy, she thought. A dish that needed a bit of preparation, something to occupy her. She trawled the meat aisle, and came up with wild boar. Brilliant! She could make a wild boar casserole for supper, from a recipe she'd been given by Lydia, Massimo's new wife.

The Englishwoman had been a chef until Gio's brother had swept her off her feet, and she'd shared lots of recipes with Anita, most of which she hadn't got round to trying. But they were elaborate enough to kill time, and that was perfect for her purposes.

She gathered up vegetables, bread, milk and a few other essentials, and made her way back to the car, feeling guilty for taking so long.

She needn't have worried. He was fiddling on his lap-top, and he shut it and put it back in the case as she got in.

'OK?'

'Yes, I was just catching up on some work.'

'You shouldn't really be doing that. You should be resting.'

'It's not exactly physically stressful,' he said drily, and she couldn't argue with him. It was pointless, she wouldn't win. She never did, not really, not a real argument. He was too clever with his words. They were his stock in trade, and she'd given up trying years ago.

Pity she couldn't give up loving him. It would make life a whole heck of a lot easier.

He went to bed when they got back, saying he needed a rest, and so she busied herself in the kitchen making the casserole.

Stupid, she realised later when he'd reappeared from the bedroom, because now supper was all taken care of and she had nothing, absolutely nothing, to do.

They hadn't even been there long enough to generate any washing, so she went and got a book from her bedside table that had been on her 'to be read' pile for much too long. But that didn't work, either. Somehow sitting there reading while he fiddled on his laptop seemed crazily intimate and settled—the sort of thing a couple did.

And they were *not* a couple, she reminded herself fiercely.

'You don't look as if you're enjoying that book,' he said, cutting into her train of thought.

'What?'

'The book. If you don't like it, why read it?'

She frowned down at it. She'd read the same paragraph about six times, and still didn't know what it said. With a disgusted sigh she threw it down and went over to the kitchen, opening the fridge and searching for inspiration.

'What are you doing?'

'Looking for something to cook.' Or something to do, more correctly. Something a little further away from him, that she had to concentrate on.

'What kind of something? I thought you'd already prepared our food? I can smell something really good, so I hope it's for later.'

'It is. It's wild boar casserole. Easy to eat with one hand. I thought I might make some chocolate mousse for dessert.'

'Can you do that?'

'Well, now, let me see—of course I can!' she retorted, rolling her eyes sarcastically.

She just needed to be able to concentrate, and that, with him in the room, was easier said than done, but she dug out Lydia's recipe, took eggs and dark, bitter chocolate and cream out of the fridge and worked her way systematically through the instructions. A few minutes later she spooned the soft, fluffy chocolate mixture into two white ramekins and smiled with satisfaction.

Perfect. And just enough left in the bowl to make licking it out really satisfying. She scooped the spatula round it, looked up and found him watching her hopefully.

'No. It's mine. Cook's perks,' she told him firmly, and stroked her tongue up the spatula.

Something flared deep in his eyes, and after a breathless second, he looked back down at his laptop and she turned away.

But the damage was done. He'd seen her licking the spatula, seen the smears of chocolate all around her mouth, and the urge to get up and go over there and kiss the chocolate off her lips was crippling him.

He kept his eyes firmly down, but even so he could see her, his peripheral vision just good enough that he could see every time she lifted it to her mouth, and finally he crumbled and looked up, just as she threw the spatula back in the bowl and plunged it into the sink.

'I hope you enjoyed that.'

'Mmm, *mmm*,' she said, licking her lips still. 'Did you want some? You should have asked. You'll have to wait now until after dinner.'

'You said it was cook's perks.'

'I might have given you a little taste if you'd asked nicely.'

Mischievous little witch.

'I'm sure I'll survive,' he said drily, stifling a smile. 'How about some coffee?'

'Again? No wonder you have dreams.'

'Wine, then? It's nearly dark.'

Wine? Sit with him and drink wine, to weaken her already fragile defences? She didn't think so.

'Have whatever you like. I'm going to have tea.'

'Make that two.'

'Please.'

He growled. 'Please,' he said, and she turned away so he wouldn't see her smiling. He was miffed because she'd eaten all the scrapings from the bowl and hadn't offered him any. Well, tough. She put the kettle on, took two mugs out of the cupboard and made the tea.

The wild boar casserole was wonderful, she thought, much better than any previous attempt she'd ever made, and he seemed to enjoy it, but the chocolate mousse wasn't quite set yet, so they left it for later.

They'd eaten at the table, because the casserole was a bit messy to eat sprawled out on the sofa, but as he went back to its welcoming softness, she could see he was struggling a bit.

'Are you all right?'

He sat down, propped his foot up and met her eyes. 'Do you know how many times today you've asked me that?'

She paused, plates in hand, and frowned. 'Oh, I do beg your pardon. I'm so sorry I spoke.'

He sighed heavily, and shook his head. 'Sorry. I'm being unreasonable.'

'You are. And it's difficult to know what else to say when it's quite obvious that you're not all right. I guess I just keep waiting for you to say you're feeling better, but you don't.'

'That's because I'm not—and I'm bored. I'm going to go crazy if I can't do something soon.'

'Like what?'

He shrugged, his smile crooked and mocking. 'We could go for a walk. Oh, no, that's right. I can't walk anywhere.'

'Ha-ha, very funny. Just remember it's not my fault, I'm not the one who hit you with the handbag.'

'Rub it in, why don't you.'

She suppressed a smile. 'Television?'

He shook his head. 'Nothing on. We could play chess if we had a chess set.'

'What, so you could thrash me?'

He smiled lazily. 'I thought you wanted me to feel better?'

'Not at my expense!'

'Anyway, it's academic. We should have thought about it earlier, we could have brought my chess set.'

'I've got one here,' she admitted reluctantly. 'You gave it to me years ago.'

He stared at her, his eyes unreadable. 'Have you still got it?' he asked softly, his voice faintly incredulous.

'Of course.'

He'd made it for her during a long, wet winter, turning the pieces on her father's lathe, carving the tops with a skill she hadn't known he possessed. He'd given it to her for Christmas, the year she turned sixteen, and although she hardly ever used it, it was one of her most treasured possessions.

She took it out of the cupboard, cleared the coffee table and set it up, and he reached out and picked up the knight, turning it over in his hand with a low chuckle. 'It took me so long to carve these,' he said quietly. 'I had to do about seven. I kept breaking the ears off the horses.'

'Is that why they look angry, with their ears laid back, so they don't stick up?'

He chuckled. 'It was the only way I could do it. The wood wasn't hard enough and they would have broken off anyway. Your father suggested it.' He put it back, a slight frown furrowing his brow as if he was miles away, back in the time when things were less complicated and rather happier.

She picked up two pawns, one dark wood, one pale, shuffled them behind her back and held them out in her fists. 'Left or right?'

He thrashed her.

She'd known he would, but he accused her of not trying.

'I am trying.'

'So focus.'

'I am focused,' she snapped. Just not on chess.

'Doesn't look like it. Try again.'

She tried. She really, really tried to concentrate, but he was sitting right opposite her with his bandaged foot up on the sofa, looking so enticing it was impossible to focus her mind on anything other than him.

And then he moved his knight and said, 'Checkmate.'

'What? How? How on *earth* is that checkmate?'

She stared at the board in disbelief, then threw up her hands and put the pieces back into the box.

'Quitter.'

She gave him a withering look and folded up the board with a snap. 'I'm not a quitter, but I'm not here as a prop for your ego, either.'

'So did you want me to let you win?'

'No! I wanted to be able to do it.' She shut the cupboard door on the offending game and stalked into the kitchen. Quitter, indeed.

'So, do you want this chocolate mousse?'

'Not if you're going to tip it on my head.'

She laughed then, letting out the frustration in a defeated little chuckle, and then took the desserts over to the table. She'd put a dollop of cream on top of each, and as they dug the spoons in, the cream slid down and puddled in the centre, ready for the next mouthful.

Gio felt the cool, creamy and yet intensely chocolaty dessert melt on his tongue, and he groaned. If sin tasted of anything, then this was it.

'Good?' she asked, and he flicked his eyes up to hers and smiled slowly.

'Oh, yes. Really good,' he said, taking another spoonful and savouring it slowly. And then he watched as she lifted her spoon to her mouth, her lips parting just enough to let it in, then closing around the spoon as her eyes drifted shut in ecstasy.

He nearly groaned out loud.

Dio, he wanted her. Wanted to taste the chocolate on her tongue, wanted to stand up and walk over to her and pull her to her feet and carry her to bed and make love to her until she screamed.

But he couldn't.

Not just because of his ankle and the cuts on his hand and thigh, but because Anita was out of bounds.

Rule number one—don't mess with friends.

He'd messed with her enough, both last night and five years ago. He wasn't going there again, wasn't risking her emotional wellbeing by letting her get involved with him again.

If he could have just taken her to bed and had fantastic and uncomplicated sex with her, it would have been fine. But he couldn't. No way. This was Anita, and nothing about their relationship was uncomplicated.

And she was a forever person, a believer in the happy-ever-after—for heaven's sake, she was a wedding planner! She made people's dreams come true.

He seemed to turn them all to nightmares.

He dragged his eyes off her, finished his dessert in silence and put the pot down. His mind full of Kirsten and the tragic waste of a life, he hadn't even tasted the last few mouthfuls. It could have been wallpaper paste.

'I need a shower,' he said curtly. 'Do you have a plastic bag and some tape so I can wrap up my foot?'

She blinked, a little startled by the sudden change of atmosphere, but this was Gio. He did this all the time, especially recently. She stifled an inward sigh and got up.

'Sure. What about your hand and your leg?'

'They'll be fine. The dressings are waterproof, apparently, so long as I don't soak them.'

She pulled a bag out of a drawer and held it scrunched up against her middle. 'Um—do you need a hand to get this on?'

'No. I can manage,' he said firmly.

'What about the tape?'

'I can manage. I can use these fingers now a little. I'll be fine. I'll see you in the morning.'

He walked out, limping heavily, shoulders ramrod straight, the bag and the tape in his left hand.

She watched him go, listened to the sound of him undressing. Grunts, the odd unintelligible comment that she probably hadn't needed to hear, the occasional thud.

Then she heard the bathroom door close, and a moment later the sound of running water.

He'd call her, surely, if he was in difficulties?

She was being ridiculous. He was fine. He was young and fit and the hospital had been happy with him. Of course he was all right.

She cleared up the kitchen, loaded the dishwasher and switched it on, wiped down the tops and tidied the sitting room. There. Now she'd go and sit on her bed with her book and wait for him to finish.

Not that she needed to. It didn't matter to her how long he took, because she had an en suite bathroom off her room. It was just that she wouldn't be able to rest until she knew he was all right.

The water had been turned off long ago, and she guessed he was drying himself. Slowly and awkwardly with one hand, she would think. She wondered how the waterproofing had worked.

And then she heard a yelp and leapt to her feet, running to the bathroom door.

'Gio? Are you OK?'

There was a stifled sound of frustration. 'I'm fine,' he said at last.

'Can I do anything?'

'Only tell me why women would ever contemplate having their legs waxed,' he growled, and the penny dropped.

He was changing the dressing on his thigh, peeling the plaster off the hairs. She winced and tried not to laugh. 'Ouch. Do you want me to help?'

'No, I want you to leave me alone. I can manage,' he snapped, and she retreated, muttering about ungracious men and telling herself at the same time that he wasn't really ungracious, he was just proud and hurt and trying to keep his distance.

And she wasn't making it any easier.

'I'll say goodnight, then,' she said, and walked swiftly away, leaving him to it. He didn't need her with him to-night. He'd had her last night, and look what had happened. From now on, he was on his own, the ungracious, sulky, temperamental—

'Stop! Stop thinking about him! Just go to bed!'

She went, exhausted from the strain of keeping up a neutral front, worn down by the emotional tension zinging between them.

And then, in the middle of the night, she had a dream...

CHAPTER FIVE

SHE was late.

They were going skiing, and she was meeting Gio at his apartment and he was giving her a lift. It was difficult, because she was dragging her skis along behind her and her bag was trundling awkwardly over the old stones, but she was trying to hurry, because he was going to be so angry with her.

She turned the last corner, hurrying towards the front door, but it was dark there, so dark, and in the shadows by the wall she could hear the sounds of a scuffle.

There was a grunt of pain, and she froze.

'Gio?' she whispered, her heart pounding. She could vaguely make out a man lying on the ground, and somewhere a long way away a woman was sobbing.

'Gio!'

'Anita—help me! I'm bleeding. You have to help me...!'

'I'm coming!' she yelled, and tried to run to him, but her feet wouldn't move. She felt as if she was running in treacle, every step a marathon, and the stones were covered in broken glass. She had to get to him, had to help him, but suddenly the place was full of people and they wouldn't let her through. They kept asking who she was, and all the time she could hear him calling her.

She began to scream, sobbing with terror. People were shaking her, shouting at her, and she tried to fight them off. She had to get to him, to help him, and they were holding her back...

'Anita! Anita, wake up! You're dreaming, *cara*! It's all right. Wake up. It's me—I'm here. I've got you.'

She heard her name, heard his familiar voice slicing through the terror and reaching out to her, and she opened her eyes and stared at him in confusion.

'I couldn't get to you,' she croaked, lifting up a hand to cradle his dear, precious, familiar face. It was warm, reassuringly so, his eyes troubled, and she felt the fight drain out of her. 'Oh, Gio, you were calling me and I couldn't get to you!' she said again, and burst into noisy, messy, uncontrollable tears.

'Oh, Anita, *carissima,* come here...'

He gathered her up against his chest, his arms wrapped firmly round her, rocking her rhythmically as he soothed her with meaningless words of comfort, and gradually the tears subsided.

He eased back, staring down at her, searching those tear-drenched, empty eyes. 'Are you OK now, *cara*?'

She sniffed and nodded, but a shudder ran through her and he knew she was lying.

'You were hurt,' she said, her voice shaking. 'You told me you were bleeding, and you asked me to help you and I tried to get to you but I couldn't run, my feet were stuck and the stones were covered in broken glass, and then everybody was blocking my way and I was so afraid you were dying—'

'Shhh,' he murmured, gathering her back up into his arms, and she slumped against his chest and let him hold her, too overwrought to care about keeping up a front. She loved him, and she could so easily have lost him. She was allowed to cry for him.

Gradually her sobs hiccupped to a halt, and her breathing slowed and eased, and he let her lie back against the pillows, her eyes staring up at him as if she still couldn't quite believe he was all right.

'I should never have let you go to my place today,' he said, his brows drawn together in a frown.

'It's not your fault. It's just my vivid imagination. It must have been seeing that piece of glass.' She shoved herself up the bed, shifting the pillows so she was sitting upright against the headboard, her hands knotted in the quilt.

She might seem all right, he realised, but she was still gripped by the dream, and the moment she fell asleep again, it would come back. He knew that. He was painfully familiar with the principle, and he was kicking himself for taking her there today.

'Hey. Why don't I make us some hot chocolate and we can sit up and drink it?'

She stared at him. 'You?'

He smiled and shrugged.

'Or I could ask you? Because you'll do it better than me.'

She gave a soft, slightly unsteady chuckle and threw back the bedclothes, slipping her legs out of bed and standing up. She was in the pyjamas again, he saw. They were meant to cover her up, but they just draped enticingly over her bottom and hugged her breasts gently, cradling them.

His hands itched to take their place, to cup her bottom and draw her closer, to feel the weight of those soft, rounded breasts in his palms once more.

'I'll just get my robe,' he said, and retreated quickly, before she could see the effect she was having on him.

Well, as quickly as he could, considering he'd almost run to her room on his damaged foot and it was giving him some significant hell at the moment.

Good, he thought as he limped hastily back to the privacy of his room. It might take his mind off Anita and her lovely, luscious body.

It didn't work.

Neither did the fact that she'd swathed herself in an ankle-length cashmere cardigan over the pyjamas. The fabric draped softly over her body, and he stifled a groan and dropped into the corner of the sofa, propping his feet on the coffee table.

'Have you got any music?'

'Mmm. My CDs are there.'

On the other side of the room.

'Just press play on the remote—it's there, on the coffee table. I can't remember what's in there.'

Jazz. Soft, smoky jazz, that filtered out of the speakers and drifted into every corner.

He leant back and closed his eyes as the lazy, haunting sound of a saxophone filled the room. It was such a sensuous instrument, he thought as the music swirled around him and through him.

Music to make love to.

He dropped his left foot to the floor and sat upright, ramming himself back into the corner and growling quietly in frustration.

'Change it if you don't like it.'

'It's fine,' he said. 'I just had cramp. I'm all right now.'

'Sure?'

'Of course I'm sure. I'm fine.'

She blinked, and then shrugged. 'Whatever. Here. Your hot chocolate.'

She set it down in front of him, and he picked it up, wrapping his left hand around the mug and propping it with the fingers of his right.

His hand was getting better, but he still wouldn't like to pick anything up with it. Two weeks, he'd been told, to allow any minor damage to the tendons to repair itself. Before then, they could tear if he over-used it, but it was too sore to want to do anything except, possibly, curl his hand gently over one of her delectable breasts and test the sweet, mobile weight of it—

He took a gulp of the hot chocolate. Too hot. He felt it scald his tongue, and he put it down again.

'Sorry, I should have put cold milk in it,' she said apologetically, settling herself in the far corner of the sofa and tucking her feet up under her bottom so she was turned to face him.

'It's fine,' he said, but his voice was a little impatient and she sighed inwardly. He really, really wasn't enjoying being cooped up with her like this—probably not any more than she was. And neither of them had needed her waking in the night from that hideous dream—

She cut off her line of thought abruptly. *Don't go there. You won't be able to sleep again if you think about it.*

'I'm sorry I woke you.'

He turned his head and met her eyes searchingly. 'I wasn't asleep.'

'Was the pain keeping you awake?'

He shook his head. 'No. I never sleep well in a strange bed for the first few nights.'

But he had, last night. Until she'd—

Stop it! Don't even slightly *think about it!*

'Well, unless I'm with you,' he added, and there it was, out in the open again, where neither of them wanted it.

'Well, I'm going to solve that for you tomorrow,' she said lightly, her voice slightly strained, 'because, after seeing your place today, I think you're probably OK to go back to Firenze. You've got the pizza place just round the corner, and you can order whatever else you need over the internet and buzz the door open. I'm sure you'll be fine.'

She glanced back at his face and his eyes locked with hers, unreadable. And then he looked away again, and nodded.

'Yes. I'm sure I will. Good idea.'

He picked up his hot chocolate, drained it even though it was still hot and stood up, yanking the belt on his robe tighter. 'I'll see you in the morning.'

And without another word, he limped out of the room and disappeared down the hall to his bedroom.

She couldn't sleep.

Every time she closed her eyes, she was back in his room with him, lying there beside him, with her hand on his chest, feeling the steady thud of his heart under her palm...

She picked up her book, but it couldn't hold her attention. She read the same paragraph she had earlier another six times, and threw it down. She was never going to get through this book as long as he was there under her roof reminding her of how much she'd missed him for the last five years.

She threw the book down in disgust and looked around.

She'd go and watch television. There probably wasn't anything decent on, and it was cold in the sitting room. February in Tuscany was not a good time to be up all night without the heating on, and she didn't want to run it unnecessarily, but it beat lying here thinking about him all night. She'd go crazy.

She got up and pulled the cardi on again, and crept out into the hall. She had to pass his room to get to the sitting room, and she hesitated at the open door.

There was a chair in his room. A comfortable, squashy armchair. She could creep in there and curl up on it and watch him. Just for a little while. He was going tomorrow, and she was going to miss him so much.

It wouldn't hurt, would it? He wouldn't even know, he'd be asleep by now, surely?

His door was wide open, the dim light from the lamp she'd left on in the hallway spilling in across the foot of the bed. She could see the lump in the bed where she'd put the cushions in it to protect his foot, and an angled lump on this side of it—his other leg, bent at the knee and turned out?

He was motionless, and she crept across the room to the chair and stopped. He'd put his clothes on it. Well, of course he had. That was one of the reasons it was in there.

So she lifted them, holding her breath so she didn't disturb him, and put them carefully down on the floor.

Something clinked against the tiles—his belt buckle? She didn't know, but she froze for a second, listening.

Nothing.

He can't have heard her, she thought, and she sat quietly down, wriggling back and tucking her feet up under her to keep them warm. And then she felt the draught from the window, and shivered and pulled the cardi higher round her neck. She wished she'd brought a throw to wrap round her shoulders, but at least the cold would keep her awake—

'Anita, what are you doing?'

His quiet, patient voice startled her, and she gasped softly. He hadn't been meant to know she was there, and she'd been so sure that he was asleep. Obviously not, or not any more.

She looked across at the bed, just as he levered himself up on one elbow and stared back at her, his features indistinguishable in the darkness. Hers, on the other hand, were clearly visible in the stream of light from the hall, and embarrassment must be written all over them.

'I'm sorry. I couldn't sleep and there was nothing on the television.' She got stiffly to her feet, the circulation cut off by her cramped position. 'I'm sorry, I'll go, I don't know what I was thinking—'

'No.' For a second he said nothing more, then he spoke again, his voice resigned. 'No. Come here, Anita. Get into bed. You must be freezing.'

She was, but still she hesitated, and then he flung back the covers on the empty side of the bed and waited.

'Well, come on. I don't bite.'

No. He didn't bite—well, not five years ago. He'd nibbled, and sucked, and trailed his tongue all over her, blowing lightly to chill the skin and then warming it again with those hot, sensuous, erotic lips—

'Is that a good idea?'

'Yes. You're cold, we're both wide awake. Just get into bed, Anita. Come on. And then maybe we'll both get some sleep.'

She closed her eyes briefly, then gave in. She knew what would happen. It was inevitable, no matter what their intentions, but somehow it didn't seem to matter any more, because the worst thing that could happen was she'd fall in love with him and she'd done that years ago.

So she peeled off the cardi and slid into bed beside him,

and he turned her away from him and hooked her back
into the curve of his warm, hard body, and covered her
with the goose-down quilt she'd never been able to bear
to sleep under alone because of all the memories the feel
of it brought back.

'Heavens, you're freezing, woman,' he said with a shudder as she wriggled her bottom closer. He wrapped his top
arm firmly round her, his damaged hand resting across
her ribs, his thumb just brushing the underside of a breast.

He tried not to think about it, tried not to think about the
times she'd snuggled up to him like this and he'd woken
her up to make love to her.

He wasn't going to make love to her. He wasn't.
Whatever his body thought to the contrary. She shifted,
and he stifled a groan and moved his injured foot out of
reach.

'Mind my leg,' he said, and she stiffened.

'Sorry, did I hurt you?'

'No.' Not in the way she meant, but to hold her and
know he couldn't have her, that he mustn't let himself
do this—it was going to kill him. 'Just remember not to
kick me.'

'I don't kick.'

He snorted softly, shifted his head so her hair wasn't
in his face and tried to zone out a little, to go somewhere
that wasn't either making love to Anita or rehashing all
the reasons why this was such a lousy idea—

'Gio? What's wrong?'

'Nothing. It's OK. I just—hell, I've missed you, Nita.'

'Oh, Gio…'

Her voice was soft, and she turned in his arms, her
hand settling lightly on his cheek, her fingers cradling

his jaw. 'I've missed you, too. We were so good together. What went wrong?'

He didn't answer. He couldn't. Not truthfully, and he'd rather not speak than lie.

'I'm no good for you,' he said gruffly. 'You need someone sensible who knows how to have a relationship. I'm a disaster, *bella*. I didn't want to hurt you, you have to believe that. And if I did, I'm sorry.'

He was. Sorry he'd hurt her, sorry she'd come to him, sorry that in the warm, soft cocoon of the bedding, there were no barriers between them that had a hope of working.

'Anita…'

It was scarcely a whisper, but the soft huff of his breath over her face, the light touch of his hand on her cheek, the gentle and inevitable brush of his lips on hers took away the last trace of her feeble resistance.

She moaned softly, and his fingers threaded through her hair, steadying her as he increased the pressure slightly. She gave in and parted her lips, welcoming the hot, velvet sweep of his tongue as he probed the secret recesses of her mouth.

'Gio,' she breathed, and he anchored her head with his hand and deepened the kiss, turning her to fire with every searching thrust of his tongue. She arched against him, her hands on his body urging them together, closing the gap until they were in contact from lips to knees.

It nearly finished him.

The feel of her body, soft, yielding, the flesh still cool and yet somehow on fire, drove him crazy, and he shoved the pyjama top out of the way and found her breasts.

So sweet, so firm and yet so soft, so real. Her breasts were perfect. So perfect, just fitting the palm of his injured hand, soothing it. He bent his head, touching his lips to her nipple, blowing lightly on it then stroking it with his tongue, and she cried out softly, her body shuddering.

So responsive to him, just as he was responsive to her. He'd never felt so much, so intensely, with anyone else, and he feared he never would.

'Don't stop,' she begged as he paused. 'Please, don't stop...'

He laughed softly in the darkness. How could he stop? There wasn't a thing in the world that could stop him now, except Anita. He touched his hand to her face, found her mouth again with his and kissed her until she sobbed with need.

'You'll have to help me,' he said at last, lifting his head and staring down at her, brushing the hair gently back from her face with his trembling fingers. 'I can't undress you with this stupid hand.'

She reached up and kissed him, her lips brushing lightly over his, their warmth filling him. And then she sat up and peeled off her top, wriggled out of the bottoms and reached for his shorts.

'Condom,' he said gruffly, checking her as she started to move over him. 'In my wallet, on the bedside table.'

She rolled away, picked it up and took it to the doorway, and he watched her hungrily as she stood naked in the stream of light and searched through it.

She hesitated at the photograph of her, momentarily distracted that he carried one, then frowned. Where would a man keep a condom?

In another pocket, zipped in. There. Several, she saw with relief, wondering why it hadn't even occurred to her to think of it. Thank God for someone with some common sense.

She threw the wallet back on the bedside table, tore off

the foil and slipped under the covers and reached for him, her fingers shaking as the tension coiled tighter inside her.

'Easy,' he murmured raggedly, and then she was moving over his body, lowering herself slowly down onto him, and it felt as if she'd come home…

Had he known this was going to happen?

He'd been so determined it wouldn't, and yet yesterday, when they'd been at the apartment, he'd gone to the bathroom and stashed a few condoms in his wallet.

Just in case.

And now he was wishing he'd brought more. A lot more.

He turned his head and looked at her. She was sleeping like a baby, flat on her back, one hand up by her face, her head tilted slightly towards him, lips parted softly.

He could see a stubble rash around her top lip, and he rubbed a hand against his jaw and frowned. It might have been better if he'd shaved last night, but by the time he'd finished the shower he'd had enough.

He'd have to be careful how he kissed her next time.

Because there would be a next time. Now they'd done this, broken down their resistance and surrendered to it, he knew there would be no going back, not until their families came home and life intruded again.

But until then—until then, they could indulge themselves, because the damage was already done.

Her eyes flickered open, and she smiled.

'*Ciao*, gorgeous,' she said, and he chuckled.

'*Ciao*, gorgeous, yourself. Sleep well?'

'Mmm. You?'

'Not really. I've been waiting for you to wake up.'

'Oh.' Her eyes widened, and she reached out her hand and cradled his jaw. 'Mmm. Stubble. Yummy.'

'Yeah. It's given you stubble rash on your lip.'

She felt it with her fingertips, and wrinkled her nose. 'Oh. That'll look good if we go out.'

'Are we going out?'

She searched his face in the dim light of dawn, and smiled slowly.

'Possibly not,' she murmured, and reached up, drawing him down to her. 'Kiss me.'

'I'll hurt you.'

'I'll live.'

So he kissed her—but not on her mouth. He kissed her neck, her shoulders, down the warm, pale slope of her breasts. He drew her nipples into his mouth one by one, sharing his attention equally so he wasn't accused of favouritism, then he moved lower, tracing a circle around the hollow of her belly button before blowing a raspberry on the soft, smooth skin just below it.

It made her gasp, and then laugh, and she could feel him smiling against her skin, feel his shoulders shift as he chuckled, the warm, damp air of his breath huffing softly across her body as he turned his head and moved downwards.

'Gio—'

'Shh.'

She bit her lips, sobbing with need, and then he moved on again, lifting her leg up so he could stroke his tongue over the back of her knee.

She shuddered and clutched at him, and he slid his hand up her thigh and stroked her with a fingertip, his head lifted now, their eyes locked.

Black, burning coals. She'd never seen such ferocious need in his eyes, and she shifted against his hand, sobbing as he teased her with the lightest touch. Then he moved up her, the rougher texture of his body trailing fire over her skin. She was shaking all over, beyond reason, needing him, needing him so much—

'Gio, please...'

He leant over her and grabbed his wallet, and seconds later he was there, entering her with one long, slow thrust, and she wrapped her arms around him and sobbed with relief.

'Anita,' he growled, his mouth against her throat, his body taut as a bowstring as he drove into her again and again. He could feel her body tighten around him, feel the shudder of her breath, feel the deep convulsions wrap around him and take him blindly over the edge into a place he'd never been before, and as he soared and fell he knew that in that moment something, somehow, had irrevocably changed...

They didn't get up that day.

Not really. They made the odd foray to the kitchen for food, and she wrapped his foot up in a bag and they showered—or at least, that was the idea. She found a garden chair and brought it in and washed it, and they put it in the shower so he could sit on it, and then they made love on the chair under the pounding stream of hot water.

Except as they came down to earth again the water was almost cold, so they turned it off and rubbed each other dry and went back to bed to warm up again until the water was hot and they could shower properly.

And then in the evening his family rang for the daily catch-up, and when he finally put the phone down he was starving.

'Let's go out for dinner.'

'What? Really? With stubble rash?'

He laughed. 'It doesn't show. I've been very careful. And anyway, we've run out of condoms.'

'Oh. Right. I'll get dressed, then,' she said sassily, but there was a hint of shyness in her smile, and a tinge of colour in her cheeks.

He laughed softly. How could she still be shy, after everything they'd done that day? There wasn't a square inch of either of them that hadn't been kissed or stroked or touched, and apart from a few concessions for his injuries, it had been just as it had before.

Well, almost as it had. There was something deeper, some new element to their lovemaking that he didn't want to think about too much.

'So, are you going to get dressed?' she asked, standing in the doorway in her jeans and boots and jumper. Her hair was loose, curling around her shoulders, and she'd put a little makeup on to cover the ravages of their lovemaking.

And he was still sitting there on the sofa staring into space and wondering what the hell was going on and what it was that was different.

'Sure.' He got up and limped back to the bedroom, pulled on his clothes with a little help from Anita at the foot end, and they headed out of the door for what felt remarkably like a date.

It was a cold, wet night, and en route to the restaurant they called in at the supermarket. The list was short. Bread. Milk. Wicked things for breakfast. And condoms. Lots of them.

They got through the checkout straight-faced, and headed back to the car laughing like naughty children. Except they didn't feel like children, and after the first two courses in the cosy and intimate little restaurant they cut short their dinner and went home to have their very adult dessert in private.

Something was different.

She didn't know what it was, quite, but there was a change in him. He seemed—not remote, exactly, but as if he was keeping something of himself back, something she'd never been allowed to see and until now maybe hadn't even been aware of.

It was almost as if he'd just discovered he had a softer side, and he was in denial. As well he might be, because if he had such a side, she'd certainly never seen it.

And yet, maybe, she had, with his nieces and nephews. His sister Carla rarely visited her family, because she lived in Umbria with her artist husband and their children, but Luca lived in the grounds of the family estate with his wife Isabelle and their two children, and Massimo, who ran the estate, lived in the *palazzo* with his three children and his new wife, Lydia. She was just a few weeks off having their first baby together, and Anita was sure Gio would be as involved with that baby as he had been with all the others.

And he was involved, for all he might deny it. They climbed all over him, sat on him and demanded stories, made him get down on the floor on his hands and knees and give them pony rides, and he did it all without protest.

Was that a man who didn't want children? Who didn't want love?

So why was he so resistant to it?

Or maybe he wasn't resistant. Maybe he was just com-mitment-phobic. She'd seen this before, with some of her brides. Their fiancés would get increasingly short-tem-pered and unsympathetic right up to the wedding, and then they'd call it all off, or make themselves so objectionable that the women called it off. Either way, Anita ended up with tearful brides on her hands, although not usually on the day.

And most of the time it was just plain nerves. Sometimes she could talk them out of it, but sometimes the stress of a wedding highlighted the flaws in their relationship.

Well, there were no flaws in her relationship with Gio, because she didn't have one. She knew that much, and this time round she wasn't going to be foolish enough to assume that this was the real thing.

Gio didn't *do* the real thing. Just sex. Amazing, incredible sex. And now it was different from before—more intense, more focused. More loving? As if, despite himself, he was giving her more than he had ever given anyone, and perhaps was getting more in return.

And sometimes, when she glanced up, there'd be a look in his eyes that she'd never seen before. He'd mask it quickly, but not soon enough to hide it from her.

She couldn't work out what it was. Confusion? Regret? Longing for something just out of reach?

Whatever it was, he certainly wasn't talking about it, so she did the only thing she could do for now and took what he gave her at face value. He'd made himself more than clear on the subject of happy ever after, and she wasn't going to push it. Not now. Not yet.

But she wasn't happy about it. For years, she'd taken anything she could, however little, because if this was all she could have of him, if it was all he was prepared or able to offer, she'd taken it, poor deluded fool that she'd been, because as the old saying went, half a loaf was better than no bread.

And where Gio was concerned, she'd settled for crumbs.

Well, not any more. Now, she wanted more. They could be happy. This interlude had proved it. And she wanted it. She wanted him, and a family with him, and the whole bang shooting match.

All or nothing, and if she had to fight for it, and she lost, then at least she'd know she'd tried, but she wasn't letting him walk away again without any explanation.

She just had to bide her time and find an opportunity to bring it up. And that, with Gio, would be no easy task.

CHAPTER SIX

NOTHING lasts forever.

He knew that, but the end of their fortnight together was coming up faster than an express train. And when the end came, their idyll would be over.

They both knew it was coming, but they both chose to ignore it.

They went to see her parents one day, and had lunch with them, careful to keep their distance from each other so they didn't give away how it was between them, but by this time they were so used to the little touches, the exchanged glances, the wordless gestures, that it was almost impossible to keep up the front, so they didn't go again. Instead they went out for drives, dined out occasionally, but mostly they were at her house doing not a lot.

She cooked for him every night, experimenting with recipes Lydia had given her, and while she cooked, humming away quietly to herself over the stove, he sat on the leather sofa and worked on his brief.

Not for long, usually, because if there was a lull she'd come and sit by him and tuck her cold toes—always cold—under his thigh, with her arms wrapped round her knees and her chin propped on top, and they'd talk.

They made each other laugh. They always had, and he'd

forgotten how much fun it was to be with her. And they squabbled about silly things; they fought over the remote control and argued endlessly about books and music, and in the evening after they'd eaten they'd play chess. Usually he won, but sometimes she did, usually because she'd cheated by doing something distracting.

Not deliberately. She wasn't that devious, but sometimes she'd pick up a square of chocolate and slowly suck it to death while she was contemplating her next move, or sit cross legged opposite him and lean over to study the board with a little frown, her arms propped on her knees and her cleavage just *there,* and he'd lose his concentration entirely and blow it.

And then she'd tease him, and he'd slowly and deliberately put the chess board away and chase her, very slowly, back to the bedroom. He still couldn't move fast, but he didn't need to. She didn't exactly run and she always, always let him catch her.

He couldn't remember ever being this happy before. He knew it was temporary, but for now, at least, it was a win-win situation, and he couldn't think of anything that he'd lost.

Yet.

That was to come, but in the meantime, they played and they loved and they were happy, and he tried not to think about the end.

Because it would come, all too soon, and he knew that this time it would hurt far more than it had ever hurt before.

And then the phone rang one morning, and it was Luca.

'Lydia looks as if she's going into labour early, so we're coming home,' he told him, and Gio felt a crushing sense of loss.

'Is she all right to travel?'

'I think so. We've just loaded the cars—could you let Carlotta and Roberto know so they can air the house and get things ready for them? They come home today.'

'Sure. Anything else you need? Food?'

'If you could grab some milk and bread and stuff, just so we've all got something for the kids, that'd be great.'

'Sure. Will do. We'll leave it in the kitchen at the *palazzo*. You drive carefully, and give our love to Lydia. *Ciao*, Luca.'

He put the phone down and met Anita's eyes. She was watching him thoughtfully, and he tried to smile, but it was harder than he'd imagined.

'They're coming home,' he said expressionlessly. 'He says Lydia's going into labour.'

She looked away. 'And they're driving for five hours? I don't envy them, the kids will be vile by the time they get here.'

He gave a humourless laugh. 'They'll be vile long before that, but they won't be stopping. They need to get home before she has the baby.'

'Is it safe to travel when you're in labour?'

'I have no idea. It's outside my experience,' he said, feeling a sharp stab of guilt and regret twist inside him. 'But Luca's an obstetrician, and he seems to have sanctioned it, so I would imagine so. I doubt they'll hang about, though.'

'I doubt it. So, do they need us to go shopping?'

He shrugged. 'Just basics.'

She nodded. 'OK. I'll get dressed.'

'Anita—'

He broke off. He didn't really have anything to say, but maybe he didn't need to say anything after all, because she

just smiled wryly and turned away, and he let out a long,
slow sigh and picked up the phone and called Carlotta.

And then he went into his room and packed.

It was over.

She'd known it was coming, known this day would be
here, but she'd counted on another three days, and she felt
so *cheated*! She'd planned things for each one of them—a
lovely drive out into the country for a picnic in the chestnut woods, then home for his favourite meal, roast chicken
stuffed with lemons and rosemary, with garlic roasted po-
tatoes and a homemade tiramisu for dessert.

A romantic, sexy DVD, with erotic little nibbles, all
aphrodisiacs designed to torment the senses and wind them
both to fever pitch. She was going to make the chocolate
mousse again and feed it to him, spoon by spoon.

Then breakfast in bed, on their last day, with the wick-
edest pastries she could find and lashings of hot coffee,
followed by some equally hot lovemaking.

And then talk. Before the others got back, she wanted
to talk to him, to discuss their relationship, because they
did have one, however much in denial he might be.

She wanted to know what it was that had kept them
apart, had stopped him from loving anyone, not just her.
Something had, surely, because he was so great with all
his little nieces and nephews, and she knew he never for-
got a birthday or a wedding anniversary, always giving
thoughtful and personal gifts.

The greatest gift he gave was his time. He was never
too busy to talk to them, never too busy to visit if it was
an important occasion, and he was deeply involved in the
family business, as well.

So it wasn't that he didn't do family. He did. Just not one of his own, and she wanted to know why.

Why he'd cut off their relationship before so abruptly was still a mystery to her. She wanted answers to that, and to why, now, he'd just taken it for granted that it would be over.

But he didn't look happy about it, so why end it?

A million questions, and as usual, no answers.

And all her plans for their last few days were wiped out in an instant. If they'd talked, if they'd hashed it all through and got to the bottom of it, and if even then he'd still wanted it to end, then they would at least have had that time, the slow winding down, a beautiful, tender farewell to their affair.

And now it would never happen.

Abruptly, without warning and before she'd had time to steel herself, it was over, the second time this had happened, and she wanted to crawl into a corner and cry.

'Are you ready?'

No crying. She was tougher than that, and this time she was going to stand and fight. She blinked, swiped away a tear that had escaped and opened her bedroom door with a smile. 'Sure. Shall we go?'

He scanned her face but said nothing, just limped out to the car with his things and put them in the boot, and he was tight-lipped and silent all the way to the supermarket. He perked up a bit for Carlotta, teasing her as she checked him over and looked at his foot and exclaimed over the bruises.

'I'm fine,' he told her, but she flapped her apron and wiped her eyes and hugged him, and then she sat him down and fed him cake. Fed both of them, because she'd looked at Anita and seen the lost look in her eyes.

'Eat! Come on, you need good food to heal.'

He looked at the slab of cake in front of him and for once he wasn't hungry. 'I've had good food. Anita's been cooking for me and she's taken very good care of me. Tell me about your grandchildren. How were they?'

'Oh, wonderful! Giovanni, you have no idea how wonderful it is to be a great-grandparent. So much easier than being a parent. You can hand them back to Mamma, and when they're clean and fed, you get them back. It's perfect!'

He laughed obediently, but Anita carried on poking the cake around her plate, unable even to smile. She was so frustrated that she'd lost a chance to talk to him, but with the family home, he'd stay here now for a while.

Maybe then she'd find a way to pin him down and find out what was stopping him, because if she couldn't change his mind about being a parent, then Gio might never know what it was to be a grandparent, because you couldn't do the one without the other.

And if he was never a parent, then she would never be, either, because after this last ten days she knew, without any doubt in her mind at all, that there would never be another man for her. She loved him so much, so deeply, that just the thought of another man touching her as he had filled her with revulsion.

'Anita, you're not eating.'

She tried to smile, but it was a poor effort. 'I'm sorry, Carlotta. I had a big breakfast, and I'm really not very hungry.'

She didn't believe her. Anita could see it in her eyes, see the sympathy, the understanding. It was no secret in the family that she loved Gio. She always had, always would, and she'd never been a good poker player. And this last week had just made it ten times worse.

* * *

Lydia had her baby three hours after they arrived back, at home, with Massimo at her side and Luca and Isabelle providing the medical backup.

They'd got back while Anita and Gio were still there, and with the baby so close it would have seemed wrong to leave at that point—rather like leaving a wedding before the bride arrived. And anyway, how was he supposed to leave? He'd need Anita's help, and she was up to her neck in children at the moment.

They were in the kitchen with his parents and the five children, Massimo's three and Luca and Isabelle's two, while Carlotta cooked up a storm to take her mind off it and the rest of them entertained the children. Francesca, Lavinia and Antonino were fizzing with excitement, but Annamaria was cranky and Maximus, Luca's youngest, was beyond tired, and so Gio battened down his feelings and picked the little boy up and rocked him off to sleep while they waited for the news.

And then shortly before five Luca came into the kitchen, a huge smile on his face, and hugged Francesca as she threw herself at him.

'Well?'

'It's a boy,' he said, beaming. 'They're both absolutely fine, and she's doing really well. Here. I took a photo. You can all go and see him in a minute.'

He showed them the picture on his phone, Francesca and Lavinia there first, then Antonino clamouring to see his little brother, and then Annamaria, Luca's daughter climbed into the fray to peer down at the picture of the smeary, streaky little baby.

'Oh, he's beautiful!' Carlotta said, looking over their shoulders and bursting into tears. *'Bellissimo!'*

He was, Gio thought, his heart clenching as he passed

his nephew back to Luca. 'Here, your son,' he said, handing over the sleeping child, and Luca eyed Gio thoughtfully but said nothing. Anita was hanging over the photo now with his mother and father, and she looked up at Gio and their eyes locked. And as he watched, the tears welled over and slid down her cheeks.

This would never be his, he realised. This happiness, this cluster of people around a hasty photograph of his brand-new baby, because there would never be a baby. The stakes were too high, the risks too great.

Pain and guilt lanced through him, and he turned away, needing to get out, done with playing happy families, and instantly Anita was at his side.

'Gio? Are you OK?'

'I need to get out of here. Can you take me back to Firenze?'

'What?' She frowned, her face puzzled. 'Aren't you going to stay here, now they're back?'

'They don't need me here.'

'They do! And you need them. You shouldn't be alone.'

'I'm fine,' he said, although he'd seldom felt less fine. He felt raw, flayed inside by all the emotion, and he just wanted to get back to his apartment and hole up for a while.

A long while.

'Well, whatever, you can't go yet. You have to see the baby, pat your brother on the back, drink a glass of something—you can't just run away!'

'Gio? What nonsense is this? You're not leaving!' his mother said, cutting him off at the pass. 'Get the Prosecco out. We need to drink to the baby.'

Luca's baby was handed to his grandmother, and Annamaria snuggled down on her grandfather's lap, and before he could protest any more he was handed a bottle of Prosecco by Luca and told to open it.

And then just as the cork popped, Massimo walked into the kitchen with the new baby in his arms, and Gio felt his heart turn over.

'They're doing girl stuff,' Massimo said with a grin. 'We've been sent out. So, *bambini*, what do you think of your little brother?'

He sat down so he was at their level, and the children clustered round him and bent over the baby, their shrill voices hushed by Francesca, ever the one to keep order between the younger ones, and Gio felt a huge lump in his throat at the sight of his brother's close-knit family.

This new baby was a huge step forward for his brother, finding happiness with Lydia after the tragic loss of his wife. It had been the year before his affair with Anita, and Gio had used the excuse that he was busy to stay away as much as he could, but in reality he'd found his pain unbearable to watch. He still felt guilty for the lack of support he'd given his brother, and now he forced himself to go over to him and do what he had to do.

'Congratulations,' he said gruffly, staring down at the tiny, precious child cradled so gently in his brother's arms. 'He's beautiful.'

The baby's eyes opened wide and he stared straight at Gio. Pain slammed through him, and he backed away. 'He's great. Gorgeous. Tell Lydia well done.'

'Tell her yourself.'

'I can't. I have to go—Anita's giving me a lift back to Firenze.'

Massimo frowned, scanning his face thoughtfully. 'Will you be all right?'

'Of course. I'm fine now. The stitches are all ready

to come out, I've just got a twisted ankle. Don't fuss. Anyway, I've got work to do.'

He nodded slowly, as if he didn't quite believe it, but the children were clamouring for attention and wanted to hold the baby, and Gio made a bid for freedom in the chaos.

'Can we go now?' he asked Anita with a touch of desperation, and she opened her mouth to protest but Luca shook his head.

'Just take him home, Anita,' he said softly, and Gio shot him a grateful look. He didn't know the facts—nobody knew, but he sensed that something was wrong, something that could never be put right, and he was cutting his brother some slack.

So Anita put his things back in the car again, and drove him back to the apartment and carried everything up for him. And then, because she knew if she didn't do it now she'd never get another chance, she tackled him.

'Gio, we need to talk.'

'No,' he said flatly. 'There's nothing to talk about, Anita. It was just a few days.'

'It was a *love affair*,' she said, her voice firm. 'I love you, Gio, and I know you love me.'

'You know nothing.'

'I don't know why you're ending it. I don't know why you ended it before. You never did explain.'

'There was nothing to explain,' he said, but he wouldn't meet her eyes. He stood staring out of the window at the distant hills, and resolutely refused to look at her.

So she left him there. He had enough food to tide him over, and as she'd told him so succinctly, anything he needed he could order in.

And then she drove all the way back to her house, walked into the bedroom she'd shared with Gio for the past ten days, curled up in the middle of the cloud-soft bedding and cried her heart out.

She thought it would get easier, but it didn't.

She resisted the urge to phone him to make sure he was all right. He had two brothers and three sisters and his parents to do that. She didn't need to get involved.

Get involved? That made her laugh. She couldn't get involved, she was already involved, right up to her neck and beyond.

She tried to bury herself in work, but curiously other people's happy-ever-after somehow didn't seem to cut it.

'You can't afford to lose business,' she told herself firmly, and rescheduled a couple of meetings for the next day, bringing them forward. She'd be ridiculously busy, but that was fine. Busy was good.

Better than sitting in the corner of the leather sofa—*his* corner—and crying.

She met with the bride she'd been with when Gio had been hurt, and of course it was all she could talk about.

'I saw you on the news, with Gio Valtieri. I didn't realise he was a friend of yours.'

'Yes. Yes, he is. I've known his family all my life.'

'They said…'

She trailed off, and went a little pink. 'Sorry. None of my business. How is he now?'

'Getting better, I understand. I'm not sure, his family's back now so they're looking after him.'

Or trying to, but she didn't imagine he'd be making it easy. He never did. He'd be grumpy and withdrawn and hostile to any offers of help or show of concern. Another reason to leave him to get on with it.

'Now, about this wedding,' she said, and dragged her mind and the bride's back into focus.

He'd gone back to the hospital at Luca's insistence for a check-up the day after he got back. They X-rayed his foot again, took the adhesive strapping off—not something he enjoyed, especially the bit above his ankle where the hair was—and then left him with a removable ankle support.

Then they took the stitches out of his hand and leg, made him move his fingers through a range of tasks, and signed him off.

He was glad about that. He'd seen enough of the hospital the first time, and the first thing he did when he got back to his apartment was have a long, hot shower. Not a good idea, because it just brought back memories of making love to Anita in the shower at her house.

Everything brought back memories, but the nights were the worst. So long, so lonely. He spent hours sitting outside on the balcony in the cold staring out at the distant hills and wondering how she was.

And then Luca came, and looked him up and down and shook his head.

'You look awful. Even worse than Anita.'

He bit his tongue so he didn't ask how she was. Not good, if Luca was to be believed.

'I'm fine. I'm just tired.'

'I can see that. You've got black bags under your eyes and you don't look as if you've eaten anything in the last two weeks.'

'One week and six days,' he correctly expressionlessly, and Luca frowned.

'Right, that's it, I'm taking you home. Go and pack your things. You're coming with me.'

'No.'

'Yes. It's not a question, Gio. Either you pack your things or I do.'

'Do what you like. I'm not coming.'

'Because Anita's there?'

He swallowed and looked away, and Luca gave a soft sigh and put his arms around him and hugged him.

'Come on,' he said, his voice softening. 'Isabelle can feed you up, and you can take over some of the office work for Massimo so he can spend more time with Lydia and the children.'

'I'm working.'

'That's not what your secretary said. She's filing her nails. She said you're supposed to be working on a case, but there's been no sign of you.'

'I'm working on it here.'

'Are you?'

He sighed and rammed a hand through his hair, the honesty that was bred in his bones not allowing him to lie. 'No. Not really.' He felt suddenly choked, and he sucked in a breath and looked up at the sky through the window.

'Let me take you home,' Luca said softly, and suddenly he couldn't fight it anymore, because he was so empty, so lost, so *lonely* without her.

He went into his bedroom, pulled out his bag and threw some clothes in it, grabbed his wash things and hesitated at the condoms.

No. He didn't need them. It was over.

He zipped the bag shut, slung the strap over his shoulder and picked up his laptop case. 'Well, come on, then, if you want to get out of here before the traffic starts.'

* * *

He was home.

Helping Massimo out, she'd heard, doing some of the company's legal work for the estate.

She found herself sitting in the dark at night and staring at the lights of the *palazzo*. Was he there? Bound to be, staying with his parents in their wing of the ancient Medici villa that was home to all of them. She wondered, now that Massimo and Lydia had taken over the larger part, which of the lights was Gio's room.

'Stop it!' she told herself when she was doing it for the fourth night in a row. 'You're being stupid. Get over him. You aren't fifteen any more.'

She moved to the chair, so her back was to the window, and there in front of her was the chess set that he'd carved for her all those years ago. She picked up one of the knights, the lovingly carved but rather angry horse so delicately detailed, and swallowed a lump in her throat. She ran her finger lightly down its Roman nose, over the flared nostrils, and remembered the times she'd won because he'd been distracted, and when she'd looked up, triumphant, there'd be that look in his eyes, the burning need, the passion simmering under the surface.

She put the little horse down, and a tear fell onto the board beside it. She wiped it away with her finger, but another fell, and then another, and she gave up and went to bed in his sheets and cried her eyes out.

And then she got up and stripped the bed at last, and threw the sheets in the washing machine and set it off before she could change her mind.

She slept in her room that night, without the memories, without the scent of him still lingering faintly on the fine cotton sheets, and when she woke in the morning she had to run to the bathroom.

Really? *Really?*

She plonked down on the travertina tiles and stared blankly across the room.

How?

They'd been so careful, so meticulous about this. There was no *way* she could have got pregnant. But she'd been feeling rough for days now, and she'd blamed it on the awful emptiness inside. But maybe she wasn't empty inside at all. Maybe...

She got slowly, cautiously to her feet, went into the kitchen and put a slice of bread in the toaster. Plain bread, a bit of dull sandwich bread which was all she'd felt like eating for the last week.

And just the smell of it toasting was enough to send her running to the bathroom again.

She waited until the nausea had subsided enough for her to eat the cold toast, and then she felt better. Slightly.

It might be a bug, she told herself, even though she knew it wasn't. She'd had bugs before, and this felt quite different. She got in the car, drove to a supermarket in the next town and bought a pregnancy test. Then she went into a café and ordered green tea, and when she couldn't stall any longer she went into the cloakroom and unwrapped the test.

Then she held her breath and waited.

One line.

Two.

Pregnant.

She laid her hand gently over her abdomen, and stared down. Gio's baby, she thought with a great welling of love, and then it dawned on her she was going to have to tell him, and she started to shake.

Well, they were going to have to talk now, she thought, and felt a shiver of apprehension.

He'd go crazy! He'd been so emphatic about it, and even though it wasn't her fault, he was going to be furious. He'd think she'd done it on purpose, to trap him. She was sure of it. He was so cynical, so wary, so untrusting of relationships, and he'd never believe it had been a genuine accident.

She could hardly believe it herself.

Her fingers trembling, she put the test back into the packet, stuffed it into her handbag and walked out through the café and back to her car. She didn't know what to do, which way to turn.

She couldn't tell her parents. They'd been unhappy enough about him staying with her, even though she'd somehow convinced them it was fine, and this would send them over the edge. They'd totally over-react, and she really wasn't up to it. Her father would go after Gio with a shotgun, and her mother would cry, and it would be a nightmare. She'd have to tell them some time, of course, but not yet.

Not now.

Now, she just needed someone who knew them both, who loved them both and could help her work out what to do.

Luca.

Relief flooded her. Luca would know what to do.

She started the engine and drove home, slowing as she passed the entrance to the Valtieri estate. Luca and Isabelle lived in the lodge just a short way up the drive, and she could see Luca's car there.

Just Luca's. Not Isabelle's. She was probably up at the *palazzo* with Lydia and the baby, and in the middle of the day there was no way Gio would be here. He'd be working in the office or out on the estate somewhere with Massimo.

She went up the drive and pulled up beside Luca's car, and he must have heard her because the front door opened and he came out.

'Anita?' he said softly, and that was enough.

His gentle voice, the kindness and concern in his eyes, pushed her over the edge and she started to cry, great gulping sobs that had him gathering her up against his side and ushering her into the house.

He led her to the kitchen, pushed her into a chair and put the kettle on, and then sat down opposite her and waited.

'I'm sorry,' she said, when she could speak again, and he just smiled and shrugged.

'Don't worry about it. You obviously needed that. Are you OK? Isabelle's out—do you want me to call her?'

She shook her head. 'No, it was you I wanted—'

She broke off, biting her lip. How could she go on? Where to start? She stared blindly at him, unable to form the words, and after a moment he sighed in realisation and gave her an understanding smile.

'Oh, Anita,' he said quietly. 'How?'

'The usual way?' she said, trying to joke about it, but it really, *really* wasn't funny. She shrugged. 'I have no idea. We were so careful—'

She bit her lip so hard it bled, but she didn't really notice.

Luca shrugged. 'These things happen sometimes. Nothing's fool-proof. I see it all the time. So—what now?'

'I don't know. I'm just so shocked. I don't know what to do—where to turn, where to go from here. That's what I wanted to ask you. What should I do, Luca?'

He tilted his head on one side, his face serious.

'What do you want to do?'

Live happily ever after with your brother?

She blinked away the welling tears. 'It's not what I *want* to do, it's what I wish I could *un*do. I shouldn't have made him to come to my house, shouldn't have insisted on looking after him. I knew it was asking for trouble, but I didn't know what else to do and I couldn't leave him alone with nobody to care for him. How could I? And now—now I'm pregnant, and he's going to hate me for it, and I just don't know how to tell him.'

'He won't hate you.'

'He will! He'll think I've done it on purpose, just to trap him, and I can't bear it. I love him so much, but he's so set against having children, so adamant that he doesn't want them, that he'll be a bad father, that he doesn't have what it takes to make a relationship work, but he's never really tried, he just walks away, every time anyone gets close…'

She tailed off, the tears welling again.

'I can't tell him I'm pregnant, Luca,' she sobbed. 'I just can't, it's the last thing he wants to hear and he's just going to go crazy…'

Luca sat back in his chair, his face grave.

'Not telling him isn't an option, Anita, I'm afraid,' he said gently. 'I'm sorry, but apart from the fact that it's shortly going to become blindingly obvious, he's standing right behind you.'

She stared at him, shock draining the blood from her head so she felt sick and dizzy.

'No!' she gasped silently. Her hands flew up to cover her face, and she just wanted to run away, to hide somewhere and wait for it all to be over, but Luca was standing up and walking past her, laying a comforting, reassuring hand on her shoulder as he went, and then Gio was sitting down where Luca had been, and his face could have been carved from stone.

'Is it true?' he asked, his voice ragged. 'You're having my child?'

She nodded, and pulled the test out of her handbag, passing it to him.

He took it, staring at it blankly as if he'd never seen one in his life before, which he might very well not have done, she thought.

'What is this?'

'It's a pregnancy test. One line is negative, two is positive.'

Two lines. Positive. Gio stared down at the test, and closed his eyes as a sea of emotions washed over him. How? How had this happened? They'd been so careful, every time. Nothing was one hundred per cent safe, he knew that from bitter experience, but...

'When is it due?' he asked, but his voice didn't sound like his and he swallowed hard, but there was a lump there he couldn't seem to shift.

'I don't know. I haven't worked it out. About seven and a half, eight months?'

He counted on his fingers, not trusting his mind with the maths. 'November? The beginning of November?'

'Probably. I can't be sure. I have no idea when it happened, but obviously in that fortnight.'

He blew his breath out slowly. He was going to be a father. Of all the crazy, ridiculous, impossible things, he was going to be a father, before the end of the year. And Anita was going to be a mother.

The mother of his child.

Shock spiralled into fear, and he swallowed again.

'We'll get married,' he said flatly. 'I'll let you fix the details. It doesn't need to be huge, just quick—'

'No.'

'No? You don't want a quick wedding?'

'I don't want a wedding,' she said, shocking him again. 'Don't be ridiculous. A few weeks ago you explained to me in minute detail that you don't do relationships, that you can't, that they always fail, that you'll be a rotten father and you'll never countenance it, and then you tell me we're getting married? I'm pregnant, Gio, not deranged. There's no way I'm marrying you because of this.'

He stared at her, another shocking possibility entering his head. 'No. You aren't planning—why did you talk to Luca?'

'Not for that!'

'Then—if you're having the baby, if you want to keep it—Anita, we *have* to get married.'

'No, Gio, we don't,' she said firmly, because the path ahead was suddenly clear and no longer so strange and terrifying. 'I won't marry a man who doesn't love me, who can't love me, who can't promise me forever—and you've made it abundantly clear that you can't. But I am going to have the child, quite definitely, and of course you can have access to it if you wish, and I hope you will, but your family will see it regularly, and so will my family, and I'll bring the baby up to be proud of his father, even if his father can't find it in his heart to love him. And I will love him, to the end of my days.'

She got to her feet, and he stood up, too, the scrape of his chair harsh in the sudden silence.

'Anita, please.'

'No. You made your feelings about being a parent crystal clear, Gio, and I won't put you in a position where you feel trapped. What kind of a marriage would that be?'

A good one, he wanted to shout, but he couldn't know that. Every relationship he'd had had failed, and the fall-out, on one occasion, had been catastrophic. What made him think this one would be any different?

And so he let her go.

CHAPTER SEVEN

HE was still standing there when Luca came back in a few moments later.

He didn't ask any questions, just walked up to him, put his arms round him and held him as the tears he'd bottled up for so long fell in a torrent.

Then he dragged himself out of his brother's arms, walked over to the window and stared out at the rolling hills. He didn't see them. All he could see was a woman's face racked with grief—grief he'd inadvertently caused. Grief that had nearly killed her.

And now it was starting all over again.

'Want to talk about it?'

'Not really.'

He sat down, not knowing what else to do, and Luca put a glass of whisky down on the table in front of him and watched him thoughtfully. He looked up and met the gentle, compassionate gaze, and sighed.

'Come on, then, let's have it.'

'What?'

'The lecture on irresponsibility.'

'No lecture. Anita assured me there was no irresponsibility. I was just wondering what's happened to hurt you so deeply in the past.'

He looked away, picked up the whisky and took a gulp. 'Nothing,' he lied.

'I don't believe you.'

'Tough.'

'Gio—you're my little brother. I know you nearly as well as I know myself. And I know when you're hurting.'

He shook his head. 'Luca, don't. Just leave it, please, and if you can't leave it, then take me back to Firenze and let me deal with this my way.'

'No. You need to be here. Anita needs you.'

'Apparently not,' he said bitterly. 'I asked her to marry me, and she said no. She said—'

He couldn't even repeat what she'd said, the words hurt him so much.

'What did she say?' Luca prompted softly.

'She said she wouldn't marry a man who didn't love her.' The words seemed to flay the skin off his heart, but somehow he carried on. 'And she said she'd bring the baby up to be proud of me, even if I couldn't find it in my heart to love him—'

His throat closed, and he picked up the glass, swirling the liquid around for a moment until he felt he had a chance of swallowing it.

'It's not true, though, is it? You do love her. You've always loved her, ever since you were fifteen.'

'Well, of course, but it's not that kind of love. It's—complicated.'

'When isn't it? That's no reason to quit, though.'

'I'm not quitting.'

'It sounds like it. It sounds like you're running away.'

He looked down into the glass, then drained it and slammed it down on the table and got up.

'This is nothing to do with Anita. And anyway, you

know nothing about our relationship,' he said roughly. 'She's just a friend—that's all. That's all she's ever been.'

'Don't lie to yourself. I don't care if you lie to me, but don't lie to yourself, Gio. She's always been more than a friend. You wouldn't be having this conversation with me if she was just a friend.'

It was true. He couldn't argue with it, so he walked out, got into the borrowed farm truck and drove away. He had no idea where he was going, but the truck seemed to know, and five minutes later he pulled up outside Anita's house.

Her car was outside. Good. He'd go in, talk some sense into her and get this wedding under way, because this was one woman he *wasn't* going to let down, one baby he wasn't going to fail, and she *would* marry him.

She wouldn't change her mind.

She flatly refused to talk to him about marriage, and she wouldn't let him in, so he sat in the truck outside her house and waited.

For hours.

She had to come out eventually, he thought, but then a cold finger of fear slid down his spine. What if she'd decided she couldn't cope? What if it suddenly all felt too much, and she did something stupid? Something dreadful—

He was out of the truck and pounding on the front door again before he had time to think, but she didn't open it this time.

What if she can't?

Fear clawing at him, he ran round to the back of the house and pounded on the French doors to the kitchen, tugging at the handle.

The lever moved, and the door swung quietly open, surprising him. He stepped inside and stopped.

She was curled up in the corner of the sofa, hugging a cushion. Her face was streaked with tears, but she met his eyes defiantly.

'This is my house. I didn't invite you in. Please leave.'

He closed the door and sat down on the chair, suddenly aware of pain in his ankle. 'No. I can't. I'm sorry, we have to talk about this.'

She threw the cushion down and got up. 'There's nothing to talk about, Gio. I can't marry you, I won't marry you, and I'm having the baby. That's all there is to say.'

'No. No, it's not. I'm not letting you do this on your own. Fine, don't marry me if you don't want to, but I'm going to be here for you every step of the way. I'm not giving up, Anita. I have every intention of being part of this.'

She scanned his face, saw the implacable expression in his eyes and the set of his mouth, and knew he meant it. Gio was nothing if not stubborn, and once he'd made his mind up, that was it.

Well, she was stubborn, too, and this was her house.

'Do you want me to call the police?'

'And tell them what? The father of your baby is insisting on looking after you?'

He had a point.

'I could call my father.'

'Have you told them yet?'

She shook her head. There was no way she was going to call her father. All hell would break loose, and she needed to feel calm and centred before she opened that can of worms.

'Please, Gio. Just go.'

'I can't. I can't leave you like this.'

'Like what? Pregnant? Are you going to sit there until I give birth, is that it? Well, newsflash, Valtieri, it takes nine months! That's another seven point something to go, and if you imagine for a moment you're going to sit there and haunt my kitchen until then, you've got another think coming. You know where the door is. Use it.'

'I can't.'

'Why?'

'Because I have a duty to you and to my child.'

She rolled her eyes and sat down again.

'Giovanni Valtieri, I've listened to you talking about your feelings on this subject until I'm sick of hearing it, and now suddenly you expect me to believe you've had a change of heart? Give it a rest. You're just trying to do the decent thing, and believe me, it's not necessary. I'm fine.'

'Are you? Are you really? Because I'm not. I feel as if my whole world has been turned upside down on its axis, and I don't know what to think or feel any more. And if you feel the same, then I'm not leaving you to deal with it on your own.'

She stared at him, slightly shocked at the sudden insight into his emotions, the closest he'd come to revealing his true feelings on anything serious for—well, forever, really. And he was right. She did feel as if her world had been turned upside down, because having his child had been something she'd wished for for years, but not like this. Not in this way, with him offering to do the decent thing and not a word of love between them.

And it made her want to cry again.

'I'm not going to marry you, Gio.'

'OK. I got that bit. But you *are* having my baby, and I can't let you do it alone. It took two of us to put it there, and there's no way I'm going to let you go through your pregnancy unsupported.'

'You can buy maternity underwear,' she said lightly, but he just looked at her, his eyes raw with a pain she didn't understand.

'Anita, please,' he said quietly, that pain echoing in his voice. 'We have to make this work. I can't tell you how important it is.'

'You could try.'

He shook his head. 'Just trust me.'

That made her laugh, but the sound echoed round the kitchen, the saddest sound she'd ever heard. 'How can you ask me to trust you when you don't even trust me enough to tell me what's troubling you? Something's gone wrong for you, Gio, I know that. Tell me what it is.'

'I can't. I can't tell you. I can't talk about it, but it was nothing to do with you, nothing you'd done. It was something I did, or didn't do. Something I should have done differently—something I can't undo.'

There was a grim finality to those words that chilled her to the bone, and in his eyes was a hollow desperation that made her bleed for him.

'Tell me,' she coaxed softly, but he shook his head.

'No. Not now. Maybe one day. But—this time, I have to get it right. I have to be there for our child, and that means being with you.'

This time? 'Not necessarily. I have no intention of denying you access.'

'But you would. If we aren't living together, then, by definition, you're denying me access to a huge part of my child's day, every day. I want to be with you during your pregnancy, to feel it move, to come with you for scans, to be there at the birth and every day afterwards. It's incredibly, unbelievably important to me. I need to be with you for this.'

She could hear the conviction in his voice, but he'd hurt her so much, and she wasn't willing to give in just because this time it was him who was hurting.

'You didn't want to be with me before,' she said rawly. 'You just walked out one morning, and when you came back, it was over. No explanation, no reasons, just—finish. Do you have any idea how much that hurt me, Gio? How much it tore me apart?'

He felt gutted by her words, reamed out inside. He'd wanted to save her from pain, and in doing so, he'd caused it, far more than he'd realised. 'I'm sorry,' he said gruffly. 'I never wanted to hurt you.'

'I thought I was going to die, Gio. I had everything I'd ever wanted there with you, and you snatched it away without any warning. And now, just because there's a child involved, you want me to let you back into my life, even though you still can't say that you love me? Why?'

The pain in her voice shredded him anew. 'Because this is different,' he said roughly. 'This isn't about want. This is about rights. A child's right to have both parents. A child's right to be safe and protected.'

'It would be safe and protected.'

'It will be. I'll make sure of it.'

He had been so emphatic about not having a child, ever, and yet now there was going to be one, he was so desperately protective of it. *This time, I have to get it right.*

What did he mean, *this time*? When had it not been right? Five years ago, when he'd done something he couldn't undo?

She felt a chill run down her spine. He'd ended their

relationship so abruptly. Could that have been the reason? Something to do with a *child*?

I can't talk about it.

Because it hurt too much?

Oh, Gio, tell me. Tell me what's hurting you. Tell me what's keeping us apart.

She closed her eyes, counted to ten and gave in.

'So what do you have in mind?' she asked, and his shoulders dropped as if a weight had been taken off them.

'I move in here, and look after you. Make sure you're all right, give you whatever you need—whatever's necessary.'

'So—just as if we were married?'

'No, not if you don't want that. I'll sleep in the other room.'

'That seems a little superfluous at this stage. We seem to have moved past that.'

They had—and yet had they? Emotionally, they were still separate entities. He'd never said he loved her, never given her the slightest suggestion of a future with him— well, not until he'd told her they'd get married, which to her at least wasn't viable without the underpinnings of emotional honesty.

And he wasn't being emotionally honest yet, not completely, or he would have told her whatever it was that had put that haunted look in his eyes. But he was trying, and moving towards it, inch by inch.

But the other room? If she agreed to that, would she ever stand a chance of getting him to open up to her? Didn't she stand more chance of that by keeping him close?

He couldn't hurt her any more than she'd been hurt already. She was beginning to think she was immune to the damage he inflicted on her every time she let herself hope, but clearly she wasn't the only one who'd been hurt.

Stick to facts.

'Your sheets are in the washing machine,' she said, conveniently ignoring the fact that they could easily be dried, 'so if you're staying tonight, it'll have to be with me.'

'I'm sure I'll cope. I'll go back to Luca's and pick up my things, and I'll be back later. And don't tell your parents without me. We'll do it together.'

'My father will want to chase you down the aisle with a gun,' she warned, and he just smiled grimly.

'Sensible man. It'll be good to have him on my side. I'll see you later. I won't be long.'

He went cross country, his first stop the *palazzo,* his family home.

He walked into the big family kitchen and found all of them, Luca and Isabelle included, gathered round the table. They looked up, and all of them fell silent.

'Giovanni?' his mother said softly, her face troubled. 'What is it? You look as if you've seen a ghost.'

He swallowed hard. How true. How very, very true.

'I'm fine. I, er—I just thought I'd come and tell you something.'

Luca got to his feet hastily. 'Hey, kids, come with me, I've got something to show you.'

'But we want to see Gio!' Lavinia cried.

'Later. Come on.'

He ushered all of the children out, and the others all turned to him expectantly. 'Well?' his father said. 'What is it? Spit it out.'

He took a deep breath, then said clearly, 'Anita and I are expecting a baby—and before you ask, we aren't getting married.'

His mother stopped in her tracks, half out of her chair,

arms outstretched towards him, and her smile faltered. She sat back down again abruptly, her mouth open. 'But—I don't understand. You love her!'

He gave a soft laugh. 'No, Mamma. I don't love her—not like that. We just—we got a little carried away.'

'And you didn't have the sense to take precautions?' his father growled.

'I did. Every time. And don't you lecture me. I know how "early" Massimo was.'

His father coloured, but his mother chipped in. 'We were engaged. You, on the other hand, are not, even though you do love her, whatever you might say to the contrary, and I'm deeply disappointed in you that you haven't got the decency to ask her to marry you.'

'Well, that's where you're wrong, you see,' he said lightly, sitting down in Luca's place and picking up his wine glass. 'Because I have asked her, and she said no.'

He filled the glass, swirled the wine around and sniffed it, held it to the light, nodded and drained it like water. Then he reached for the bottle again, and Massimo's hand came out and removed it.

'No. You're not sitting there and getting drunk. What are you going to do next?'

'Pack and move in with her. She won't marry me, but she's allowing me to look after her.'

Isabelle frowned. 'That doesn't sound like Anita.'

'It isn't. I didn't give her a choice.'

Massimo snorted. 'I'll bet. I don't suppose you thought to *tell* her that you love her?'

'Will you all give up with this? I don't love her!' He got to his feet and walked to the door. 'You know where I'll be if anyone needs me for anything. I'll see you tomorrow.'

* * *

The door was unlocked when he got back there with his things, and he walked in, calling out her name.

She didn't answer. She was wandering round the kitchen with a piece of toast in her hand, looking grim.

'I feel sick,' she said. 'I thought it was morning sickness. I've been feeling sick all day.'

'Ring Isabelle. She'll have some tips. Or Lydia.'

'I thought you were going to look after me?'

'I am, but I've never been pregnant, Anita, so I can't tell you what will make it better. However...'

He sat down, got out his smart phone and started searching.

'Carbs,' he said. 'Lots of carbs. Never let yourself get hungry or dehydrated. Keep your blood sugar up. Fruit and plain toast or crackers.'

'Done that. It doesn't work.'

'Stress is bad for it.'

She gave a short, bitter laugh. 'Oh, well, that's all right then, I'll just chill out, shall I?'

He put the phone down and stood up again, walking over to her and pulling her reluctant body into his arms. 'I'm sorry. I'm so, so sorry. I really didn't want this to happen—'

'You think I don't know that?' she asked slightly hysterically, pushing away from him and heading for the biscuit tin. 'Ginger biscuits. I bought some the other day—'

'Want me to go shopping?'

'No, I want you to go, but I'm not going to get my wish.'

She found some plain biscuits, the sort that were best dunked in hot coffee because otherwise they were pretty flavourless. Perfect. She curled up on the sofa and nibbled the edge of one, and gradually the nausea subsided again.

'Better?'

'Slightly. If I could work out what I need, it would be better. I feel really hungry.'

'What have you eaten today?'

'Biscuits. Toast. Not much.'

He nodded, and walked into the kitchen and started opening cupboards.

'What are you doing?'

'Cooking for you.' He pulled his phone out of his pocket and rang Luca. 'What do I feed her?'

'Pasta or boiled rice with butter and salt. Oh, and green vegetables. Clean flavours. No meat, Isabelle says. Lydia says anything she doesn't see again in five minutes is good. Stir fry with fresh ginger in it and soy sauce. And they send their love.'

He gave a wry laugh and opened the fridge. 'OK. I can do something like that. *Ciao.*' He put the phone down and turned to her.

'They send their love. You ought to talk to them.'

She sighed. 'I ought to talk to my mother, but I feel so grim.'

'Let me feed you, then we'll talk to them.'

He pulled out vegetables—leafy greens, sprouting broccoli, peppers. He shredded them, dry-fried them in a touch of oil, put them on a bed of buttered boiled rice and added a slosh of soy sauce.

'Here—try that.'

She recoiled, but tasted it, chewed, swallowed and went back for more, and he blew out a silent breath and cleared up the kitchen. He'd made enough for two, but by the time he'd finished it he was wondering if he'd survive. He was starving, and the whole dish had lacked any kind of richness—entirely the point, of course, but it wasn't going to get him through the next few weeks.

There was some leftover pasta and sauce in the fridge, and he sniffed it. It smelt amazing.

'It's fine. I made it yesterday and couldn't eat it. I thought I might feel better today. Just—please don't heat it.'

Because it would bring out the smell. He nodded, stuck a fork in it and ate it cold, then he put the plate in the dishwasher and went over to her, perching on the edge of the sofa next to her.

'OK?'

She nodded. 'Yes. Thank you. I was just hungry, I think. I feel much better.'

'Better enough to tell your parents?'

She closed her eyes and rested her head back. 'They aren't going to understand,' she said wearily.

'They need to know. It's not fair that the others know and they don't.'

'How do the others know? Did Luca tell them?'

He shook his head. 'No. Luca would never do that. Patient confidentiality and all that. I told them. I hope you don't mind.'

She shrugged. 'It's your baby, too, Gio.'

He glanced down, and noticed she was sitting with one hand lying gently on her abdomen, cradling it. She'd be an amazing mother, he thought with a sudden rush of affection, and vowed to do everything in his power to keep her safe. It was beyond him to make her happy. Keeping her safe—them safe—would be enough of a challenge.

Her parents were delighted.

She was the last of their children to have a baby, and they'd almost given up on her, and so they were thrilled about that, if not about the situation. They were a little shocked because this had come almost out of nowhere, but the fact that they'd spent time alone together wasn't lost on them; they'd seen them together in that time, and she didn't think for a moment they'd managed to disguise the intense chemistry between them.

Not that there was any sign of it now, of course.

Gio was polite, friendly, solicitous—and driving her gently mad. He also made it abundantly clear to her parents that not getting married was her idea, not his.

Clever move, but he wasn't a lawyer for nothing, she thought wryly. Manipulating people's emotions was all part of the job, and he was highly successful at his job.

He took her home—well, she drove, but only because he was in the borrowed farm truck and it was a bit basic. But he ushered her out to the car, opened the door, closed it and went round and sat beside her and fastened her seat belt, even though it was only a few hundred yards on private roads.

'How about a nice relaxing bath?' he suggested, and she nodded.

'I'll go and run it.'

'No. You eat something. Luca said you need to eat constantly. Little and often.'

He went to run the bath and came back to find her munching salty potato sticks out of a giant packet.

He stole a few, put the kettle on and made her a cup of hot water with a slice of lemon and a sliver of fresh ginger—her mother's suggestion—and then chivvied her into the bathroom.

She was glad to be chivvied, if she was honest. She was exhausted, and it had been a deeply emotional and stressful day. And it wasn't over yet. They had the night to get through, and she'd had to put his sheets on to wash again because they'd been left in the machine overnight and she still hadn't tumble-dried them. Sort of deliberately, because she wanted him to be with her so she could catch him when his guard was down and find out what was really going on, but now she was beginning to regret that.

A little privacy might have been nice—time to lie and contemplate the enormous change that was coming in her life, not least the inextricable inclusion in it, for the foreseeable future, of Gio Valtieri—but that was never going to happen. Not for weeks, if not months.

She knew enough about him to know that when he'd made up his mind, it was made up, and he wasn't going anywhere until he was ready.

There was a tap on the door.

'How are you doing?'

'OK. I was about to get out.'

'Can I get you anything?'

Peace?

'No, I'm fine.'

She heard him walking away, his gait slightly uneven still. It had been better, and she wondered what had happened to make him limp again. She'd noticed it earlier. It was only five weeks since his attack, and he'd healed better than she'd expected, but maybe not as well as she'd thought.

She climbed out of the bath, got dried and dressed in her snuggly, full-length bath robe, then emerged from her bedroom to find logs burning cheerfully in the fireplace and Gio sitting with his feet up and his laptop on his lap.

He shut it down as she went in and got to his feet.

'OK?'

'I'm fine. Gio, please, stop fussing. I'm pregnant, not sick.'

'Sorry.' He didn't sound sorry, he sounded implacable, as in, 'I'm sorry, but that's the way it is, live with it' sorry.

'Were you working?'

'No. I was looking up the early stages of pregnancy.'

She shouldn't have been surprised. This was Gio, after all. He made it his business to be informed on any subject that was relevant to him or his work, and this, the slow and systematic creation of a living being from next to nothing, would be tackled no differently.

'How many weeks are you?'

'I don't know. Between seven and five, I guess. You go from the first day of the last period.'

She felt herself colouring—absurdly, since it was a perfectly normal thing and he had to know all about it, but that was fact and this was *her*, her body, her system, her cycle. And that made it somehow weird, despite the fact that he knew every single inch of her body because he'd spent almost two weeks very recently mapping it in minute detail.

'And that was?'

'I don't know. Sometime before we were due to go away. I can't remember exactly. It's not really relevant, I just get on with it. I know I should have been all right for the holiday.'

He nodded, and she could see his brain working.

'I just wish I knew how it had happened,' he said quietly. 'What went wrong, what we did or didn't do.'

'It doesn't matter now, though, does it?' she answered. 'The result's the only thing that really matters. Are there any of those potato chips left?'

They went to bed early.

She was exhausted, and she fell asleep on the sofa and woke up with her head on his shoulder. Strange, because he hadn't been sitting there, he'd been in the chair, and yet now he was next to her, his arm around her back, her head cradled comfortably in the hollow of his shoulder as he rested back beside her.

She stretched and sat up straight, rolling her head on her neck, and he retrieved his arm and stood up.

'Bedtime?' he murmured, and she nodded sleepily.

She needed the loo again, and she was hardly able to stay awake. How could anyone miss the signs, she thought, because her body was screaming out to her that something had changed, something was different, and she couldn't possibly have missed it.

She fell into bed, and a few moments later he joined her, settling himself down on the far side of the mattress, giving her space. It felt curiously lonely, and she knew she was being perverse but she wished he'd hold her, because she could have done with a hug.

'Did you put the fire guard up?'

'Yes, and I checked the doors were locked. Relax, *cara*. Go to sleep.'

He lay there listening to the sound of her breathing. It was slightly uneven, interspersed with the occasional sigh, and he knew she was still awake. Worrying about the future, or about them? The two were now linked, of course, and the thought made him go cold inside.

What if he let them down? What if he failed Anita, or worse still, failed the tiny and incredibly vulnerable child cradled in her body?

He couldn't fail again...

'Gio?'

He turned his head, and saw her looking at him in the dim light from the hall. 'Yes?'

'Hold me?'

Her voice was soft, a little tentative, as if she thought he might reject her, and with a soft exhalation he gathered her close and held her gently in his arms. He wouldn't fail her. It simply wasn't an option.

'It's OK, Anita,' he said, his voice slightly unsteady. 'It's going to be all right. I'll look after you.'

He would. She knew he would. She just wondered if he'd ever let her look after him, because someone needed to. The look on his face just now had been harrowing to see.

Grief?

She sensed a deep well of sadness in him. She had no idea what had happened, but something bad enough that he still couldn't talk about it, and she was horribly afraid that it involved a child.

He'd never mentioned it until today, but some time after their affair had ended Luca had told her that he didn't know what was wrong with Gio but that something big must have happened. Something tragic and heartbreaking?

And now, he was holding her as if she was the most fragile and precious thing in the world, and it made her ache inside. If only he could trust her—trust anyone. But he held himself aloof, and always had.

Everybody's friend, and yet nobody, not even his brothers, really knew him.

She laid her hand on his heart, snuggled her head down closer into the hollow of his shoulder, and let exhaustion claim her.

And as she slept, Gio kept watch over her, and knew that somehow, somewhere, he'd find the strength to do this, because he had no choice. Because it was Anita? Would he have felt like this about any other woman, or would he simply have made some tidy financial settlement, settled custody and access arrangements and left it at that?

Maybe, but Anita was different. Anita had always been different, and he'd never been able to keep a sense of perspective about her. And now there were three of them to pay the price because he hadn't been able to keep a sensible emotional distance between them, but had succumbed, not once, but twice, to the lure of the fairy tale that seemed to dangle in the air just out of reach whenever he was with her.

Well, it was in reach now. All he had to do was make damn sure that Prince Charming didn't turn back into a frog.

CHAPTER EIGHT

SHE had to give him credit where it was due.

For a man who knew nothing about pregnancy, who claimed that he was useless at relationships and didn't have any sticking power, he did a very passable impersonation of the ideal partner.

She woke up that first morning still in his arms, and lay there for a few minutes luxuriating in the warmth and intimacy of a totally platonic embrace. It might not have stayed that way, but for those few moments, while he was still asleep and she was feeling OK, it was wonderful.

And then the nausea hit, and she leapt from the bed and ran.

She thought she was going to die, kneeling on the cold stone floor wondering how on earth she had got herself in this mess, and then suddenly, unexpectedly, a warm, strong hand appeared and held her hair out of the way, the other hand lying gently on her shoulder offering silent support.

She sagged against his legs, and he stood there, soothing her with a rhythmic sweep of his thumb against her shoulder, waiting until everything settled down, and then he handed her a hot, damp flannel to wipe her face, and disappeared.

She got up and rinsed her mouth and followed him

into the kitchen, just in time to be handed a slice of toast smeared with yeast extract.

How did he know that? How?

She ate it ravenously, demanded more, and then snatched it from him the moment it was spread.

'Good, eh?'

'Amazing,' she said with her mouth full. 'Thank you.'

'Don't thank me, that was Lydia. Tea?'

'Mmm,' she said warily. 'Maybe. Decaff? Not strong, very little milk?'

It was perfect. Under normal circumstances she would have thrown it down the sink, but on that day—that day it was just right.

And so it went on.

She tried to work, but it was difficult. She made some phone calls to brides, pulled together a few ideas, but she just felt so *tired* all the time, and when she wasn't stuffing carbs, she spent a large part of every day napping.

And every time she woke he was there, tapping away on his laptop, writing up a brief or emailing a colleague.

'I'm going to trash your career,' she said, but he just smiled.

'I don't think so. I was due some time off. This is just routine stuff.'

She nodded, and got up to put the kettle on. He was at her side instantly.

'Hungry?'

'I could eat something. I could always eat something. Pasta? No dairy. Something clean flavoured.'

'Arrabiata?'

'I haven't got any sauce.'

'Well, isn't it a good job I got some?'

She propped herself up against the worktop and watched

him slice the vegetables. 'You know, for someone who's so rubbish at relationships, you're pretty good at this domestic stuff,' she said softly, and he glanced up and met her eyes.

'Just doing my bit,' he said lightly, but there it was again, that lingering shadow, the ghost of some remembered sadness in the back of his eyes.

'Gio, what's wrong?' she asked, catching him by surprise, and he cut himself.

He swore softly, grabbed a piece of kitchen paper and squashed it firmly on his finger. 'Nothing. What makes you think anything's wrong? Apart from the fact that I've cut myself. Do you have any plasters?'

'Sure.' She let it drop and went and found him one, wrapping it firmly round the end of his left index finger. 'Do you want me to finish cutting that up?'

'No, I'm done,' he said, scraping it into a pan and setting it on the hob, and he couldn't have told her any more firmly that the subject was off limits.

He had to go back to Firenze the following day.

Because she'd pushed him too hard? She didn't know, but she missed him. He got a lift in with Luca, and was driving himself back when he was finished, but then he called her.

'I'm going to be late home,' he said. 'Camilla Ponti wants to see me.'

'What!' She was stunned. More stunned that he seemed to be considering it. 'Are you going to see her?'

She could almost see him shrug. 'She can't do me any harm. Apparently she wants to apologise.'

'Or convince you not to prosecute her for assault,' she said sceptically. There was a long pause.

'Perhaps. I don't know. Anyway, I won't be back till much later. I'm sorry. Will you be all right?'

'Of course I will, Gio. I might spend the evening with Massimo and Lydia—get in a bit of baby cuddling for practice. It might remind me what it's all about when I feel queasy. Light at the end of the tunnel and all that.'

'Sounds like a good idea. I'll call you when I'm on the way home. You take care, *bella*. I'll see you later.'

He hung up, and she rang Lydia, arranged to go round there and spent the evening cuddling little Leo.

He was delicious, the most gorgeous baby she'd ever seen, and Lydia was more than happy to talk babies and share her top tips for morning sickness and all the other joys that were to follow.

Isabelle came up, too, and they spent a wonderful girly evening together while Massimo went down to Luca and babysat his two and left the girls to it.

But always, in the back of her mind, was Gio.

He'd said he'd ring when he was leaving, but it was almost ten by the time she went home, and there had still been no word from him, so in the end she rang him.

It went straight to voicemail, but she didn't leave a message. What was she supposed to say? 'Where are you?' She wasn't his wife, she didn't *want* to be his wife—not under the terms he was offering—and she wasn't going to behave like one.

So she went to bed, and she lay there and worried about him anyway.

'Signore Valtieri—thank you so much for agreeing to see me. I realise I had no right to ask.'

He shook her hand and pulled out a chair for her.

'Signora Ponti. Please, have a seat. I gather you want to apologise?'

'Yes. But I need your help, and I don't know where else to turn.'

His help? He stared in shock at the broken, dishevelled woman across the desk from him who sat wringing her hands. He'd expected contrition of some sort, but this was beyond anything he'd imagined, and it just underlined his feelings at the time of the attack. She'd been so desperate, so distraught. And she was now.

'I'm not sure how I can be of help to you.'

'I want you to ask Marco to help me. He won't see me.'

'I'm not surprised. I thought we'd said all there was to say at our meeting. Why you felt you had the right to come after me and assault me, I have no idea. I know you didn't mean to hurt me that badly, but I could have died because of what you did—why should I listen to what you have to say? And why on earth should I help you?'

She closed her eyes, and a tear squeezed out from under one lid. An act? Maybe—and maybe not.

She opened her eyes and looked at him, and he could see the pain in her eyes all the way down to her soul. It shocked him. This wasn't acting, this was a woman on the edge of a precipice.

'I can never apologise enough for what I did to you,' she said softly, her voice shaking. 'I'm not even sure what I did do. I don't remember hitting you. It was like a red mist came down over me, and I just wanted to lash out at you for what you'd done to me.'

'I did nothing to you. You had no case, I demolished it. It was obvious what was going to happen.'

'No. There was nothing obvious about it, not to me. The

only obvious thing was that I had to try. Signore Valtieri, do you have a child?'

He went still, motionless, but beneath his ribs his heart was pounding. 'No,' he said, knowing it was only part of the truth yet not willing to share his private pain with this woman.

'Then you won't understand what it's like to love your child so much that you'd do anything for him, even lie and cheat and steal, just to keep him safe.'

She opened her hand, and flattened out the photograph that was clutched in it. She laid it on his desk and pushed it towards him.

'This is my son.'

She slept fitfully, unable to relax completely until he was home, and then finally, at nearly one in the morning, he let himself in.

He didn't come to her room. She lay there for a while, listening and waiting, and then finally, unable to rest without knowing if he was all right, she got out of bed, pulled on her robe and went to find him.

He was sitting on the sofa in the dark, staring out over the distant valley. Most of the lights had gone now, the headlights of a vehicle moving slowly along the winding roads the only sign of life.

He heard her come in, and he turned his head and held out a hand to her. '*Bella.* I thought you'd be asleep. Come and sit with me.'

He patted the sofa cushion next to him, and she came and curled up beside him, tucking her feet under her bottom and snuggling into his shoulder.

'You're late.'

He was. His meeting with Camilla Ponti hadn't been at

all what he'd expected, and he'd spent most of the evening trying to work out what to do from now.

'Yes. I didn't mean to wake you. I'm sorry.'

'You didn't. I wasn't asleep. I tried to ring you.'

'I know. I'm sorry I didn't answer. I was thinking.'

'That hard?'

She could see his mouth twitch, just slightly, into what might almost be a smile, but it was a smile that tore at her heart. She reached up and laid a hand on his cheek.

'So how was she?'

'She wanted to apologise,' he said gruffly. 'She's fallen apart, Anita. She looked horrendous. Initially when we had our meeting all those weeks ago she was pretty self-contained at first, and you could imagine her as a successful business woman. She was elegant, smartly dressed, composed—well, until she realised she would lose. Today—what can I say? She was untidy, she looks as if she's aged twenty years and she couldn't stop crying.'

'Sounds like a good act.'

'No,' he said quietly, 'it was no act. She was genuinely distraught. She told me she needed the money because her child's in a care home. He suffered injuries in a car accident before he was born, and she can't look after him, he needs specialist care. That's what she needed the money for, why she stole from Marco for years, and why she needs her half of the business. To support her son.'

'And you fell for this?' she asked, incredulous, but he just smiled sadly.

'She showed me a photograph of him. He's a teenager now, but he can't speak and he can hardly move and it's an absolute tragedy. And before you say it, I know it's true, because after she left I checked up on it.'

Anita sighed, racked with guilt for doubting the poor

woman. 'Gosh, Gio, I'm sorry. It just sounded so implausible—how dreadful for her. For him—for both of them. Doesn't she have a husband to help support her?'

'No. He died in the car accident. It turned out he wasn't insured, so there's no compensation and the cost of his care falls entirely to her. That's why she cheated Marco all those years, and then tried to get her half of the business, to cover her spiralling debts. And when it was obviously not going to happen, it pushed her over the brink.'

'I should think it did. Oh, how awful. So how will she pay his care home bills?'

'She can't, and she's got a lawyer's bill she can't pay. And he's putting pressure on her.'

'Who represented her?'

'Bruno Andretti.'

'Did he know what it was for?'

'I don't know. It doesn't matter, she had no way of winning and he should have told her that. I wonder if he knew about the fraud? If she didn't tell him, it's not his fault. I'll go and see him, see if I can sort it out. And I'll talk to Marco. He doesn't know about the child. If she didn't tell her business partner, I doubt if she told her lawyer.'

'Is he a friend of yours?'

'No, but I know him. He's OK.'

He shifted so he was facing her, and laid a hand gently on her cheek, his eyes tender. 'You look tired, *cara*. Come on, back to bed.'

She fell asleep almost instantly, cradled in his arms, and he lay there holding her and thought of their child, of how he'd feel if anything happened to it. The surge of raw emotion shook him, and he wondered how it would feel to be Camilla Ponti, to have no way to help your child and no money to pay the bills, with your life falling apart around you.

He couldn't let it happen to her, to them. He'd talk to Bruno, and he'd talk to Marco, and see if he couldn't sort something out for her.

He went off again the next day.

'I don't know when I'll be back, but it shouldn't be too late,' he said as he left her at the door.

At the last second he leant in and kissed her, just a gentle brush of his lips on her startled mouth, and then he drove to Firenze and went to see Bruno.

'I'm afraid he's busy,' his secretary said.

'Tell him it's Giovanni Valtieri.'

She disappeared through a door, and came back a moment later looking surprised. 'He'll see you now.'

'Thank you.'

He walked through the door she'd gone through and closed it softly.

'Andretti.'

'Valtieri, *ciao*—come on in. Coffee?'

'Thank you.' He took the cup and set it down. 'I want to talk to you about your client, Camilla Ponti.'

Bruno sat back in his chair, propping one foot on the other knee and rocking slightly on the spring, a smile lurking in his eyes. 'Ah, yes. Are you better now? I heard you fell over a refuse bag. Careless, that. I take it you want to sue? Because you won't win.'

'No, thank you for your concern. I want to talk to you about your bill.'

He frowned. 'My bill? What about my bill?'

'I'm surprised you didn't tell her she had no case. Did

you know anything about her? Did you find out why she needed the money? Why she had debts?'

He dropped his foot to the floor and leant forwards. 'I didn't know she had debts. She told me nothing—only that Marco Renaldo had refused to give her her share of his company.'

'Because she'd embezzled funds from him, because she needed the money. She has a son with severe disabilities. He's in a care home. It's very expensive, but he needs specialist care.'

'She didn't tell me any of this. Am I supposed to be a mind-reader?'

'No, but you could have checked her credit rating,' he said drily. 'However, it's not too late to help her.' He picked up his coffee cup from the edge of Bruno's expensive plate glass desk and took a sip. 'I want you to waive your fee.'

'What? Don't be ridiculous—'

'I'm not being ridiculous. I'm waiving mine, and I'm going to ask Marco to help her. I know you don't have to, but it would be a gesture you can well afford.'

He stroked the surface of the desk with an idle finger, and Bruno gave a short huff of laughter.

'You owe me lunch.'

'Any time. Just not today, I have a lot to do.'

He drained his cup, shook Bruno's hand and drove straight to see Camilla Ponti.

'Your lawyer's agreed to waive his bill,' he told her gently, 'and I've paid your son's overdue fees and the next quarter to give you breathing space.'

Her eyes flooded with tears. 'But I attacked you,' she said, confused and unable to believe him. 'I could have killed you. Why would you do that for me?'

He smiled sadly. 'I didn't tell you the whole truth. I

don't have a child yet, but I will, in a few months, if all goes well. So, yes, Signora Ponti. I don't agree with what you did, but I *do* understand. And I want to help you, so that you can be there to support him.'

It still wasn't the whole truth. There was more, but it was too private, too painful and not for her ears, and so he left her then, promising to be in touch, and drove home to Anita.

It was time to explain, to tell her what had happened, and to ask her to try and understand why it was that he couldn't dare to let her love him.

She was asleep, curled up on the sofa, her hand under her cheek. She looked so young, so innocent, and he felt a wave of guilt that he'd hurt her all those years ago.

But wasn't that what he was doing now? He was no good at love. He always failed, always bailed out when it got messy or complicated. By staying with her, wasn't he putting her at risk of falling in love with a man who couldn't ever seem to deliver?

Dio, he wanted to, so much, but he wasn't sure he could. Every time he'd tried, he'd failed. He couldn't let himself fail Anita. Better not to let her ever rely on him emotionally. Physically, for practical and financial support, yes, of course. But for love?

He didn't think he had what it took, however much he might want it, but maybe he owed her that explanation. It was just finding the way to tell her that seemed so hard.

She stirred, and he crouched down beside her, brushing the hair out of her eyes.

'*Ciao, bella,*' he said softly, and her eyes flickered open.

'Gio—you're home.'

Home. The word sliced through him, and he sucked in

a quick, light breath. So welcoming. So dangerous an illusion…

'*Si.* I was done early. Can I get you anything?'

'Tea? I'm so thirsty. I keep trying to drink water but it just makes me feel rough.'

'Do you need to eat?' he asked as he put the kettle on.

She nodded. 'Probably. Not toast, though. I'm off toast.'

He found a packet of plain sea-salted crackers and put them down in front of her. 'How about these?'

She took one and nibbled the edge of it, and nodded. 'Lovely. Thanks.'

He was in a suit, she realised. Sharp suit, crisp white shirt, a silk tie she thought she recognised. Power-dressing. Why? Business meetings, of course. He must have been back to his apartment and picked up some more things.

'Successful day?'

He propped himself up against the kitchen cupboards and smiled slowly. 'Yes. I persuaded Bruno Andretti to waive his fees for representing Camilla.'

'You must have been quite convincing.'

'I was.'

Of course he was. She ran her eyes over him. The suit was immaculately cut, skimming his taut, muscular frame and subtly emphasising his masculinity. Power dressing, indeed. He looked amazing in it, and just looking at him made her mouth water.

'Go and change, and then come back. We need to go shopping. I meant to go earlier, but I fell asleep, so there's nothing to eat tonight. Go. Shoo.' She picked up her tea, grabbed another cracker and settled back on the sofa to wait for him.

They went to the supermarket and picked up a few things, and then while she curled up on the sofa in front of the television he fried chicken and cherry tomatoes, piled them in a dish and baked it in the oven while they watched the news, and then he served it with a bowl of penne pasta tossed in light olive oil and basil.

He'd stirred some mascarpone through his, because the bland and inoffensive chicken cacciatore was missing the soft and creamy cheese, but he hadn't wanted to risk cooking it which might bring out the smell. He'd learned quite early on that smell was one of the main things that set her off, and he'd taken to visiting Massimo in his office for coffee in the mornings for that reason.

'Yummy,' she said, cutting off another piece of chicken. 'This is really good. I had no idea you could cook so well.'

'Of course I can cook. You really think Carlotta let us grow up without knowing something as essential as how to feed ourselves? We can all cook.'

'Did you leave the mascarpone out?'

'Only from yours. I didn't want to upset you. Did you want it?'

'No. It's great. Just right. I was a bit worried when you said what you were cooking, but I might have known you'd get round it somehow. I'm sorry, you must be so bored with my dull diet.'

'It's not that dull, and I'm sure I'll survive, *cara*,' he said softly, and he wanted to scoop her up in his arms and kiss the guilty little smile off her face. Just in time to tell her—

Oh, this was so hard.

He cleared the table, made them a drink and sat down beside her.

'No. Go the other side. Let's play chess. I could do with a mental challenge, it might wake me up.'

He lost. He lost two games running, and then put the set away, his heart pounding.

'Why are you doing that?'

'Because I can't concentrate. I need to talk to you, Anita. There's something I should have told you years ago, something you need to know.'

Finally.

She sat back against the sofa and searched his face. His expression was serious, his eyes troubled. She patted the sofa beside her.

'Come here,' she said softly. 'Whatever it is, we can deal with it.'

He hoped so. Oh, how he hoped so, but he was very much afraid she was wrong, because there was a flaw in him that he didn't think even Anita could fix.

And he didn't dare risk giving her that chance, because in trying to fix him, she could end up broken, and who would fix her? Not him. He had no skills in that department. His only skill seemed to be in doing the opposite, and he'd passed that one with flying colours.

CHAPTER NINE

HE sat down beside Anita, put his arm around her and drew her in to his side.

He was tense, his whole body taut, and she snuggled closer and slipped her arms around him. 'Hey, relax, this is only me,' she said quietly. 'Whatever it is, it won't change what I feel about you. Just tell me, and then we'll talk about it.'

She made it sound so easy—but maybe it was. Maybe he just needed to say it.

'It was just before our affair,' he began, and she felt her heart start to pound harder. She'd known it was something to do with that time. Maybe now, finally, she was going to find out why they'd split up. He'd gone to work one morning with a tender kiss and a promise for later, and when he came home that evening, he told her it was all over. No warning, nothing. Finished. And she'd been devastated.

'It was September, and the weather was glorious,' he went on. 'I had a brief affair, with a girl called Kirsten. She was Australian and over here studying art history. She was based in the Uffizi at the time, and she was bright, savvy and we had a fling. Only she didn't think it was a fling, she'd thought it was much more serious than that. I'd kept it light, she never came to my apartment and I never spent the night with her, but somehow she fell in love with me anyway.'

Somehow? Anita nearly laughed, except she knew just how poor Kirsten felt. Falling in love with Gio was painfully easy.

'I don't know how she managed to convince herself it was more,' he said, sounding genuinely perplexed. 'I was very careful to keep it simple, as uncomplicated and casual as possible. I really, really didn't lead her on, because I didn't want her to think I was offering more than I was. It was a pleasant enough interlude, she was a lovely girl, we had fun, but that was all it was, Anita, all it was ever meant to be. So I ended it, as gently as I could, and she got upset. There was nothing else I could do, I didn't love her, I wasn't going to marry her, and I felt I'd made that quite clear all along, but she didn't want to hear it.

'She stalked me for a while until I told her firmly to leave me alone, and then she gave up and I assumed she'd got over me and moved on. And then I went to your brother's wedding, and you were there, of course, and we had rather too much to drink and danced all night. And the next day we went back to Firenze, and I took you out for dinner, and then afterwards I took you back to my apartment and made love to you for the first time.'

He touched her cheek, his eyes sad. 'It was amazing. I'd wanted to do it for so long, and it was better than I could ever have imagined. And we had fun, didn't we? Lots of fun. We did all sorts of silly things, and we spent every spare minute together, and it was great. And then one day I had a letter, at work, from Kirsten's parents. She was in hospital in Adelaide. She'd seen us together, apparently, and she'd flown home, got some pills and taken an overdose.'

'Oh, Gio, no!' She'd known something shocking was coming, but not this. She reached up, tracing her fingers over his face, seeing the lines of grief etched in his skin. 'Oh, I'm so sorry. Did she survive? Was she all right?'

'Yes. Yes, she survived, and she was expected to make a full recovery, but she told her parents she'd wanted to die because she couldn't get over me, and then after she'd been admitted to hospital the doctors realised that she was pregnant.'

Pregnant? Anita's fingers stilled against his face, and her hand dropped to her lap. She'd wondered, but...

'You've got a child?' she asked numbly.

'No. That's the worst thing.' He sucked in a ragged breath. 'She lost the baby, Anita,' he said, his voice hollow. 'She lost the baby because I couldn't love her the way she wanted me to. She really shouldn't have got pregnant. I was careful—so careful—but maybe she sabotaged that in an attempt to keep me. Or maybe it wasn't even mine. I don't know. She said she didn't realise she was pregnant when she took the pills, and I have no way of knowing if that's the truth, but it makes no difference. She tried to kill herself because I let her down, and so a baby died because of me, and I will never forgive myself for that.'

'No.' She couldn't let him believe that. She couldn't believe he did, it was so far off the mark. 'A baby died because its mother let herself believe in something that wasn't true. You hadn't egged her on, made her false promises, told her you loved her. You didn't tell her you loved her?'

'No! No, of course I didn't. It wouldn't have been true.'

'So you hadn't led her on, but nevertheless she'd painted a happy-ever-after for the two of you that was never going to happen. Trust me, it's easy to do. I know that. It's what I did in those few short weeks when we seemed so happy.

But then you came home one day, with no hint, no clue, no warning whatsoever, and told me it was over. Was that the day you got the letter?'

He nodded slowly, his eyes filled with regret. 'Yes, that was the day I got the letter. I didn't know what else to do. I was stunned, on auto-pilot, and the only thing I could think was that I had to end it before you had a chance to convince yourself you were in love with me, and certainly before you became pregnant. But you've already told me how much I'd hurt you, and you were painting happy-ever-afters, so I was already too late,' he added, his voice strained.

'Oh, Gio,' she said with a tender smile. 'It was always going to be too late. I'd been doing the same thing every time you noticed me since I was fourteen and my hormones kicked in. Only this wasn't just noticing me, it was much, much more than that, and because we seemed so happy, I let myself fall even deeper in love with you.' She shook her head. 'Gio, why didn't you just tell me about her when you got the letter? You tell me everything, but you didn't tell me that. Why not?'

He shook his head. 'I don't know. I just wanted to protect you, in the only way I knew how, which was to get you away from me as quickly as possible before I could hurt you, too.'

'Why did you think you would hurt me?'

'Because I always hurt everybody. I've had a rule, for years, not to get involved with nice girls. Only sleep with women who know the rules. And rule number one, don't sleep with your friends. And you were my best friend, Anita, and I'd broken my rule. And I thought if you fell in love with me, at some point it would get messy and I'd want out, because I always did, and I was afraid you might do the same thing as Kirsten, only you might have been more successful. I couldn't have lived with that, with the knowledge that you'd died because I'd let you believe that I was in it for the long haul. So I had to make it clear there was no long haul and never would be, because I don't seem to be able to do it.'

'Maybe you've never let yourself try.'

'I have. Of course I have. I gave up trying, years before Kirsten. She just caught me unawares, and she just proved what I'd known all along. I'm a lousy bet, Anita. I hurt every woman I touch.'

'Will you tell me something? Honestly? How many times have you told a woman you love her?'

He stared at her blankly, then looked away. 'Never.'

'Because you've never loved anyone, or because you've never committed to it?'

'I've never loved anyone. I don't seem to be able to. I like them, I'm fond of them, I enjoy their company, but none of them make me feel—'

Like you.

He nearly said it out loud, but he was glad he hadn't, because it took his breath away.

Was that it? Was the reason he'd never loved anyone before because none of them had been Anita?

'Maybe you've never let yourself love, Gio. Maybe it's never mattered enough to try and make a relationship work, and so you've never let your guard down before. Perhaps there's never been enough at stake before, and maybe now you should, because there is. There's a lot at stake here, Gio. Maybe it's time to try.'

He met her eyes, aching to believe her, but the thought of hurting her was anathema to him. 'What if I fail, Anita?' he said, his voice strained. 'What if this all loses its gloss and we end up hating each other? I'll break your heart, and I couldn't bear to do that.'

'No, you won't. No more than you have in the past. And anyway, we won't hate each other. No more than we already do. And if you're worried you'll get bored, I'll have to find ways to make it entertaining,' she said with a gentle, slightly mischievous smile.

She reached up and touched his cheek with the backs of her fingers, her caress tender. 'Gio, you can't hurt me, not unless you're deliberately unkind. I've loved you forever, and nothing's going to change that. And if we can make this work, for ourselves and for our child, isn't that better than never having the courage to try?'

He swallowed. 'I don't know,' he said after a long hesitation. 'I seem to have this fatal flaw, and I don't know if I've got what it takes. And I'm so afraid I'll hurt an innocent child. You're an adult. I worry enough about hurting you, Anita, but our baby—I couldn't hurt our baby. I've already got one child on my conscience. I can't have another.'

His words echoed in her head, going round and round.

I've already got one child on my conscience. I can't have another. Can't have another. Already got one. Can't have—

She sat back, realisation dawning. 'Is that why you're here?' she asked, shocked. 'Why you've insisted on looking after me? Because you're afraid I'll do something foolish and harm the baby? Gio, *never!* I will never, *ever* harm our child, or myself. I feel desperately sorry for your Kirsten, but I've spent my whole life knowing that you'll never love me the way I love you, and I'm not going to suddenly do something foolish because I've found out I'm pregnant, any more than you are.'

'Me?'

'Well, yes. Why not? I won't marry you under these

circumstances, and I've told you that, but I never for a moment thought you'd go off and try and kill yourself because of that. I know you better, I know your strengths, and you really ought to know mine.

'I'm tough, Gio. I can do this alone, and I will if necessary, but I'd much rather do it with you by my side, and if you find you can love me, if you find that our relationship is different to all your others and you want to stay, then maybe we *could* get married. In the meantime, I'll carry on, and you'll have to decide for yourself what kind of a relationship you want with me, long or short term, and I'll do my best to go along with it, because come hell or high water, we're going to be together in some form over this. We've got a child to bring up, and it's down to you whether we do it separately or together. And the only way to find out if we can do it is to try.'

He stared at her, and let his breath out in a whoosh. 'Really? You'd do that—take that big a risk, for me?'

It was the biggest gamble of her life, but she had no choice. If she was ever to win Gio, to convince him that he could love her, then she knew instinctively that this was her only chance.

'Why not?' she said gently. 'What have I got to lose? I *love* you. And if you give yourself a chance, who knows, maybe you can love me, too. But you have to try, or you'll never know.'

Could he trust himself enough to try? Trust her? He wasn't sure. What if she suddenly realised she wasn't as strong as she thought? What if it all fell apart and she found she couldn't take it and wanted out? If he let himself love her...

But if he didn't try, if he didn't let her try, then they'd lose it all anyway. Life had no guarantees.

'OK,' he said, feeling the ground fall away from under his feet. 'We'll try—but I'm not promising anything, Anita. I've never stuck at this in my life, and I'm thirty five. That's a long time to spend moving on.'

'I know. And we'll take it step by step, and I won't put any pressure on you, I promise. Let's just see what happens.'

Her eyes were gentle, her face so close he only had to move his head a little way for their lips to touch.

She met him halfway, her breath easing over his face in a soft sigh as their lips met. With a ragged groan he gathered her into his arms and kissed her as if she was the most precious thing he'd ever held, and deep inside her, she felt a glimmer of hope spring to life.

She knew he loved her. All she had to do was wait for him to realise it, too.

Sliding her arms around his neck, she kissed him back, kicking it up a gear, and with a groan he shifted her in his arms and stood up, carrying her to the bed and laying her down in the cloud-soft bedding.

He took her clothes off slowly, item by item. Her sweater. Her jeans, already too tight so that the stud had to be undone. Her bra, also on the small side now. The tiny scrap of matching lace that barely covered those soft, moist curls.

She was exquisite, and he wanted her so badly he thought he'd die. He stripped off his clothes, shucking off his jeans and shorts and socks in one movement, and then rolled back to her, gathering her into his arms again and covering them to keep out the chill.

He kissed her all over, paying homage to every inch of her body. He hesitated for a moment, his lips pressed low down against her abdomen, close to their child, and he vowed to do his best to make this work, for all their sakes.

She touched him gently, her fingers threading through his hair in a tender caress. 'Gio?'

He shifted back up the bed, cradling her head in his hands and kissing her deeply. He had to have her, had to make love to her before he went crazy, and he was about to reach for his wallet when he stopped himself. Not necessary. She was already pregnant with his child, and that brought a whole new dimension to their lovemaking.

It was the first time in his life he'd made love to a woman without a barrier between them, and the physical sensation was incredible, but the emotional connection was even stronger. And as he lay with her afterwards, cradling her gently against his heart as their breathing returned to normal and their heart rates slowed, he knew that nothing he'd ever experienced before in his life could touch this.

Was it love? He didn't know. Whatever it was, it was the most beautiful, most terrifying thing he'd ever experienced, and it left him deeply shaken and humbled and more determined than ever that this was going to work.

It had to. The alternative was unthinkable.

The next few weeks were the most amazing and nerve-racking of his life.

When he wasn't working on the estate or in Firenze, he looked after her, cooking for her to make sure she ate sensibly, going out for short walks to make sure she got some fresh air. And when he was working, he sent her texts, and flowers, and left notes for her inside the fridge.

He spent more and more time working in the family business alongside Massimo, taking over some of the admin and marketing work. This freed his brother up to do what he really wanted to do, which was experiment with new varieties of grapes and olives, to improve and expand their range of products, but it also meant he could go home to Anita for lunch, and sometimes lunch stretched into the afternoon...

March turned into April, and the weather was glorious. They got the cushions out of storage and put them on the benches around her loggia, and in the afternoons they lay there bathed in the slanting sun and read books and dozed.

And at night, they made love.

But still, he held something back, because he wanted to be sure, didn't want to say 'I love you' until he could be certain he meant it. Not when the stakes were so high.

And Anita waited, but the words just didn't come.

No matter. He did love her, she was more sure than ever, and she could wait. She'd waited decades. Another few weeks weren't going to kill her.

She went to see Luca, one day when Gio was in Firenze. She rang him, and he was at home, so she went to speak to him about managing her care during her pregnancy.

'How's it going?'

She smiled. 'OK. Gio's being amazing.'

'Yeah, he's around a lot. How is that?'

She felt herself colour. 'Good. Well, some of it. Luca, I've tried to convince him to give himself a chance to make this really work, but he can't believe that he can really love anyone. I don't know if he ever will.'

'That's ridiculous. Of course he loves you.'

'I know, but it's not that simple.' She hesitated, then she said, 'There was a woman, an Australian. Something happened, something I can't tell you, but it's made him so wary. It's as if it's broken something inside him.'

'Well, if anyone can mend it, Anita, it's you. I knew

there was something. I'm glad he's told you. I have no idea what it is, but he needed to talk about it, and I'm glad he's trusted you with it. It's a good sign.'

'I hope so. Luca, about the baby. Isabelle and Lydia tell me I need to sort out my maternity care and I'll need a scan, they said. Can you sort it for me, or at least point me in the right direction?'

He smiled. 'I knew you were going to ask me that. I'd rather not look after you myself, it's a bit personal and you might not want to look at me over the dinner table afterwards, but I'll get someone on my team to supervise your care, and if you're OK with it, I'll make sure I'm up to date with your notes so you can ask me anything you aren't sure about.'

She nodded, and he went on, 'You'll need a scan at about twelve weeks. I take it you're still a bit vague on your dates?'

She gave a wry chuckle. 'Well, I can tell you the only dates I could have conceived, if that helps pin it down. There's a ten day window, right smack in the middle of your holiday. Stick a pin in it.'

His mouth twitched. 'That'll be fine. I'll get the paperwork done and book you an appointment at the right sort of time. We'll be able to give you a pretty exact gestational age from the scan measurements. Anything else?'

'No. I'll leave you to get on. I know you're up to your eyes in paperwork, because Isabelle said you were. I'm sorry if I've held you up.'

He hugged her warmly. 'You haven't held me up at all. It's a pleasure to talk to you, Anita. It always is. And for what it's worth, I'm delighted you're having my brother's baby. It's about time something normal and adult happened to him. He's spent far too long chasing a lifestyle he doesn't even like.'

It was an interesting remark, and she wondered which bit of his lifestyle Luca was referring to. The work, as a lawyer? Or his love life—actually, scratch that. Not *love* life. Social life? Private life? Better. More accurate.

She tried not to think about all the women who'd been in his life. She hadn't been a nun, exactly, but there had been very few men in her life, and none of them had had a prayer of living up to Gio. And since their affair five years ago, there had been no one. If she couldn't have Gio, she didn't want anyone, and she'd officially resigned herself to being an old maid.

She went back to her house and checked her phone for messages. Oops. Some of her brides were getting antsy, and she made a few phone calls, set up some meetings and decided she really, really ought to tell the ones who were booked for later in the year that she wouldn't be available to run their wedding days, even if she was able to set everything up for them at this point.

She mentioned it to Gio when he got home, and he pulled off his tie, dropped into the corner of the sofa next to her and put his feet up on the coffee table.

'Cancel them. Tell them you aren't going to be available if you don't want to do it. *Do* you really want to do it?'

Did she? 'I'm not sure,' she said slowly. 'Some of them are just spoiled brats who want every last thing going, and I hate arranging celebrity-style weddings for empty-headed little girls who don't seem to think at all about the real meaning of marriage, but some of them—some of them are just lovely, and when it's really important to them and I can give them the day of their dreams, it's just fabulous.'

'So cherry-pick,' he said, as if it were that simple, which

maybe it was. 'You won't need the money, I've got more than enough for both of us, and you'll have plenty to do when the baby comes. Do as much or as little as you want.'

'You don't mind if I work?'

He laughed softly. 'Do I have any say in it? I'm not your husband, Anita, and I'm certainly not your guardian. It's entirely up to you what you do with your life. But no. Of course I don't mind. But before we go much further down the line, we ought to talk about where we're going to live.'

'We?' she said tentatively, but he just shrugged.

'You, then, at any rate. You and the baby. Will you stay here, or do you want to live in Firenze?'

So not we, then, she thought and felt her spirits nose-dive. 'Why not here? It's got everything I need and my family are close by.'

'It's a little small. We could do with another bedroom or two, and I was thinking the area beyond the loggia would be perfect for a swimming pool. I can just see it now—an infinity pool, with nothing beyond but the valley. Gorgeous. Fantastic.'

She laughed softly. 'Gio, I don't have that sort of money to spend.'

'But I do,' he said, his voice quiet and sincere. 'The pool is just a bit of nonsense, but the bedrooms—well, it would be nice to have it all done before you have the baby. You don't want the dirt and disruption afterwards.'

He was talking about investing his money in her house. Buying into the relationship? It sounded very much like it. Very much like commitment, but still there was no sign of those little words she was waiting for, and he couldn't seem to settle on 'we' or 'you'.

'By the way, Camilla Ponti's going to be OK,' he told

her, catching her by surprise. 'I've spoken to Marco, her ex business partner, and he's going to take her back.'

That surprised her. 'Just like that?'

He laughed. 'Well, not quite. He had no idea she had a child with disabilities. She'd never said anything about her private life, and so he had no idea what she was dealing with in terms of her finances or the personal stresses she was under. So he's taking her back, in a different role, for a small fixed salary which will be just enough to live on, and he's going to pay her son's fees for as long as she behaves. And if it goes well, she gets a pay rise.'

'Wow. That's impressive. How did you talk him into that?'

He gave a wry smile. 'I took him to the care home when she was there, and she introduced him to her son. He came away in tears.'

'Have you met the boy?'

He nodded, his smile fading. 'Yes. And I have to say, the staff there are amazing, and it's worth every cent of what she pays. He's very limited in what he can do, but they can tell when he's responding and they communicate with him far more than I would have thought they could. And so he's contented, which is more than I would have expected considering the level of frustration he must feel.'

'That's so sad.'

'It is. It's incredibly sad.' He held his arm up, making space for her next to him. 'Come here.'

She scooted over, snuggling in next to him, and he laid his hand over the little bump that was now beginning to show.

'*Ciao*, baby,' he said softly, giving her bump a gentle stroke with his fingers. 'You doing all right in there?'

'Seems to be. I went and saw Luca today, and he's going

to book me in for a scan for around about the twelve week mark.'

'May I come?'

She took her gaze from that gentle, caring hand and looked up at him. There was a curiously diffident expression in his eyes, as if he wasn't at all sure of her answer, and she hugged him.

'Oh, Gio, of course you can. It's your baby, too.'

His mouth flickered into a smile. *'Grazie,'* he murmured, and kissed her.

She laid her hand over his. 'I hope the baby's all right,' she said softly, her fears for it coming to the surface now after their conversation about Camilla's son.

'So do I, Anita, but if it isn't, if there's anything wrong with it, it won't make any difference. I'll still love it. You were wrong about that, you know. It's not that I can't find it in my heart to love our child, rather that I don't trust myself not to let it down, but until you were pregnant I don't think I really understood what it meant to be a parent. Not in a personal way. I understood the physical responsibility, and the need for emotional security, but I didn't understand what it would feel like to know that your child is slowly growing and developing, turning into a real person that's part of you. I do now, and I know that whatever happens to us, I could never walk away from this.'

'Oh, Gio.'

She tilted her head and stretched up, pressing a kiss to the rough plane of his jaw, and he turned his head and found her mouth and kissed her lingeringly.

'Are you hungry?' he asked. 'Do you need to eat soon?'

She smiled against his mouth. 'No. I've been eating biscuits all afternoon.'

'Good. Because I have something else in mind for you

right now,' he said with a cheeky grin that reminded her of the boy she'd first fallen in love with. He pulled her to her feet, took her out into the hall and turned right instead of left.

'What? Where are you taking me?'

'It's a surprise,' he said, and ushered her out of the front door.

He took her for a picnic to the chestnut woods on the Valtieri estate.

They parked the car and he got a wicker picnic hamper out of the back and threw a blanket over his shoulder and they followed the path down to an opening in the trees. The valley stretched out in front of them for miles, and they could see the *palazzo,* and Luca and Isabelle's house, and nestling in the trees was her house, with her parents' much larger villa just beyond.

'I love it here,' she said, settling down onto the picnic blanket with a contented sigh and wrapping her arms around her knees so she could see the view.

He dropped down beside her, lying out full length and folding his arms behind his head. 'You always did. If ever I couldn't find you and there'd been a ruckus of some sort, I'd know where you'd be.'

'I still come here sometimes, when I feel crowded or I need to think about stuff.'

'So do I. We spent so much time in these woods when we were kids. Do you remember?'

She lay down beside him, and he put his arm out so she could use it as a pillow. 'Of course I remember. I remember you falling out of that tree over there and breaking your leg, and I had to ride your bike down to the *palazzo* and try and find someone to help get you down, and you were so cross because you said you could have sat on the bike and freewheeled down.'

'I could have,' he said with a smile.

'And if you'd fallen off? You would have made it far worse and your mother would have killed me.'

He chuckled. 'Very likely. Do you remember when I crashed the bike into a tree?'

'Yes. You were so badly winded I thought you'd never breathe again.'

'*You* thought that?' he said, laughing. 'I thought I'd lie there and slowly suffocate, waiting for my lungs to re-inflate. It was a nightmare. I never did tell my parents about that.'

She smiled and laid her hand over the baby. 'I wonder if it's going to be a boy like you,' she said, and pulled a face. 'It'll be a nightmare to bring up.'

'I'm sure we'll cope,' he said, and there it was again, the 'we' word, hanging in the ether.

He pulled her closer, and she lay there in the crook of his arm and rested her cheek on his chest and wondered what the future held for them.

CHAPTER TEN

'I've got my scan appointment through.'

He hung up his jacket on the back of a chair and took the letter out of her hand. 'I'll see if I'm free. If not, I'll have to shuffle things.'

He sat down next to her, kissed her absently and pulled out his smart phone. 'OK. Here's my calendar. Yes, I can do that, I think. I'll have to move a client, but that's fine. Is this the clinic's address?'

'I think so.'

He nodded, tapping it into his phone. 'OK. You ought to have this calendar on your phone, so you know where I am at any time.'

She blinked. 'Why would I need to know that?'

He shrugged, and she smiled and leant over and kissed him, reading his mind. 'Nothing's going to happen, Gio,' she said. 'I'm fine.'

'Nevertheless, you might need to know where I am, and I'd like to know where you are. Do you have a virtual calendar?'

'Of course I do. I use it to keep track of all my weddings and meetings. I'd be lost without it.'

He hesitated for a second, then said, 'Want to swap passwords?'

She stared at him. This was a big thing for him. It didn't sound like much, but to give her access to his every movement, and to ask for hers—that was a real investment for him. 'Sure,' she said slowly. 'I'll get my phone.'

It made sense. She could see that. She was just amazed that *he* could, that he'd feel it was necessary to share all his movements with her—unless he wanted to be able to keep tabs on her because he was still worried she'd do something foolish. Either that or he wanted to know how much she was doing so he could interfere and tell her to cut back.

Or maybe, she thought, it was just as he said, that it made sense to know what both of them were doing.

They swapped passwords, so she had his diary as well as her own on her phone, and she could update it daily. And then he made her put his number in her phone as the emergency contact number.

'Just in case. You never know. I've put you in as my contact now.'

Not his parents? Not one of his brothers?

Wow. She put her phone away, and went into the kitchen and started to prepare supper, still thinking about that.

'Hey, are you feeling up to cooking, or do you want me to do it?'

'No, I'm fine with it. I'm feeling better. Not brilliant, and I won't be brewing coffee or cooking cheese any time soon, but I might let you have meat again.'

He laughed, his eyes crinkling as he looked up at her from the sofa, and she went over to him and bent and kissed him, just because she could. She couldn't believe he'd put her in his phone as the emergency contact—

'You need some more clothes,' he said, staring appreciatively down her cleavage as she straightened up. 'You're beginning to blossom.'

'Is blossom a euphemism for getting bigger breasts?' she asked drily, and he chuckled.

'It might be. And your tummy's starting to show when you stand up.'

'I don't think it's anything to do with the baby. I think it's all the relentless carbs I've been eating.'

He got up and followed her back to the kitchen, sliding his hands round under her arms and cupping her breasts gently. 'Mmm. Whatever, it suits you.' His hands slid down, linking together over her tiny bump and easing her back against him, and he bent his head and nibbled her neck.

'Will supper keep?' he asked, his voice muffled, and she turned in his arms and smiled at him.

'I'm sure it will. What did you have in mind?'

'Oh, a little this and that.'

But his eyes were smouldering, and as he lowered his mouth to hers, she reached behind her and turned off the oven. Some things didn't need to be hurried…

He shifted his client, and got home in plenty of time to take her for her scan. She was drinking water all the way there in the car, following her instructions.

'I hope they don't keep me waiting too long,' she said wryly, but they didn't keep them waiting at all. Luca was there, and he greeted them both with a hug.

'Do you want me to go, or may I stay?'

'Stay,' Gio said, not even giving Anita a choice in the matter, because he was suddenly afraid for the baby and if there was anything wrong, he wanted Luca there to talk them through it.

Funny, he'd never thought of it before, but Camilla Ponti's son had brought home to him with vivid clarity just how badly things could go wrong, and it had only been then, meeting the boy and realising the depth of her commitment, that he'd realised what they'd inadvertently signed up to with this pregnancy.

What any couple expecting a baby signed up to.

'Anita?'

Luca, checking with her. She was nodding, and then she was lying down on a couch, undoing her too-tight jeans and sliding them down just far enough. She reached out her hand, and Gio gripped it, staring at the screen as the person wielding the ultrasound wand began to scan her.

'There we are. That's the head, the spine—and see that? Fluttering? That's the heart beating.'

He felt Anita let out a breath, and he squeezed her hand. The scan moved on, checking other things—the position of the placenta, verifying that there was only one baby, taking measurements for the dates.

Early. Early in their ten-day window—that second night, when they'd made love so hastily, so urgently? She'd torn open the foil with shaking hands. Had she damaged it? Maybe. He'd been too shot away with need and longing to notice, but it seemed irrelevant now, looking at the grainy and yet somehow extraordinarily clear image of his child.

'That all looks really good,' Luca said from behind him, and he rested a hand on his shoulder and squeezed it hard. 'There. You can both relax now.'

'Want a photo?'

'Yes, please,' they both said at once, and Gio asked for two. One each, so he could have one in his wallet and carry it everywhere with him.

She got off the couch and disappeared to the cloak-room to get rid of the litres of water she'd drunk, and Luca

slung an arm round his shoulders and led him out to the
waiting area.

'So. How does it feel?'

'Amazing,' he said, staring down at the photo in his
hand. It blurred suddenly, and he had to blink hard to clear
it. 'Absolutely amazing. I can't believe it's happening.'

'Oh, it's happening. You wait. It'll feel like ten minutes
and you'll be woken up first thing on a Sunday morning
by a child arriving on the bed with a great big smile and
a story book.'

'Are you trying to put me off?'

Luca smiled and hugged him briefly. 'I wouldn't dream
of it. You enjoy it. It's fantastic. Right, I have to go, I've
got a clinic, but it's good to see you and I'm glad everything looks OK.'

'Thanks, Luca. For everything.'

He smiled and nodded, and left him there staring at the
image of his baby. Was it conceived that night? It had been
the night he'd made love to her for the first time in five
years, and in that moment, right afterwards, he'd somehow known that everything had changed.

Was that how Kirsten had felt, the night their baby had
been conceived?

*Oh, Kirsten, I'm sorry. I didn't mean to hurt you. I never
meant our child to die.*

'Gio? Are you OK?'

He pulled himself together and smiled at Anita, suddenly realising just how OK he was. The past was past. It
hadn't been his fault, he hadn't taken the drugs, he hadn't
known she was pregnant, he had nothing to blame himself for. And now, he had the future to look forward to.

'Yes, I'm fine,' he said, blinking away the sudden tears.
'You?'

She smiled back, her face serene. 'Never better. Shall we go for lunch?'

'Good idea. Here, your photo.'

She tucked the envelope in her handbag and took the one he was looking at out of his hand.

'I wonder what it is?'

'Does it matter?'

'No. No, not at all. I just think a girl might be slightly less worrying to bring up.'

'Only until puberty,' he said drily, and ushered her out of the clinic.

He stood at the window of his apartment in Firenze, staring out over the distant hills and contemplating his future.

His life was changing drastically, and everything about it was good. The baby was doing well, and they seemed to be getting on fine.

More than fine. Brilliantly well. He was happier than he'd ever been in his life, and she was blooming. He couldn't imagine it getting any better, and he knew, without a shadow of a doubt, that he would never tire of her. How could he when he loved her so much?

He loved her? Well, of course he did! He'd been gradually accepting it for weeks, and yet he'd never voiced it in his thoughts, never formalised it.

But yes. He loved Anita Della Rossa, with all his heart and soul, and he always had. No wonder his relationships had always foundered. They'd all been with the wrong woman.

It hit him like a thunderbolt, and he sat down abruptly. He loved her. He really, really loved her. Not just as a friend, but—how did it go? Truly, madly, deeply? He smiled, and then he laughed, and then he got up, left the apartment and drove home.

She wasn't there.

Odd. He'd checked her calendar, and she wasn't supposed to be doing anything this afternoon, unless something had come up since he'd synchronised it last night.

Maybe she'd decided to go shopping, or have lunch with the girls, he thought, disappointed that she wasn't at home when he had to tell her this vital and amazing thing, and he tried to ring her, but it rang and rang, and then went to voicemail.

OK. Maybe she was busy. He'd try her later.

Still nothing. He left a message.

'I'm back home. Call me. I've got something to tell you.'

He went to see Massimo, and found him in the kitchen surrounded by his family.

'Can we have a quick word?'

'Of course.' He stood up, kissed Lydia in passing and ushered Gio into his office. 'What's up?'

'I've been thinking,' he said, getting straight to the point. 'You've got more than enough to do here, and hardly any time for your family. I already do all the company's legal work, and there's plenty more I could usefully do, like the stuff I've been doing. How about taking me on permanently?'

Massimo frowned at him, then blew out a long breath. 'Really? You'd dump your law practice?'

He shrugged. 'Maybe not entirely. But I'm sick of it. I've had enough of juggling people's lies, and it's time to look out for my own family. I'm going to be a father soon, and if Anita'll have me, I'm planning on being a husband. I don't want to be stuck in Firenze while they're here, and I've really enjoyed working with you. I think we could build the business, play to our strengths, find other areas to expand into. What do you say? Do you think it's viable?'

His brother stared at him for a long, long moment, then let out a huff of laughter. 'Oh, yes. I definitely think it's viable. Papà and I were talking about it only yesterday, wondering how we could persuade you away from the sinful city.'

He smiled. 'I need no persuading. I just have to convince Anita that she'll have me. Do you know where she is, by the way? I thought she'd be at home, but she's not, and I can't get her. I wondered if she was with Lydia or Isabelle, but her car isn't at their house and it's not here, either.'

'Shopping? I know she had a meeting this morning, because Lydia rang her, and she said something about going on to do a bit of clothes shopping while she was in town. Try her again. She was probably just somewhere noisy. And, yes, by the way. It would be great to have you on the team.'

'Good. Let's hope you're still saying that in a year's time.' He grinned, slapped Massimo on the back and left him, pulling out his phone as he ran down the steps to his car.

He called her again, left another message, and went home. She still wasn't there, and he began to get worried.

Her meeting had been just outside Chianciano, and there were good shops there, but surely by now she'd be on her way home? He rang her, and got her voicemail again.

'Anita, where are you? I'm starting to get worried. Call me.'

He'd give her half an hour. And in that time, he'd do the intelligent thing and go into her calendar and update it, just in case.

Nothing. No changes.

So where was she?

He couldn't drive there and look for her along the road, that was crazy. There were two routes, one via Pienza and Montepulciano, the other the quiet back road that ran through the forest and nature reserve. That was her most likely route, he thought, and the one where if she'd run out of petrol or broken down, she was less likely to be helped by a passing motorist. She couldn't change a puncture now, not while she was pregnant, so she'd be sure of having her phone on her. So why wasn't she answering it?

His mouth dry, he rang her again. 'Anita, please, call me! I don't know where you are, and I think something must have happened. Please, call me, *cara*. I love you.'

He hung up, beside himself. He'd have to try and find her. He picked up his phone, set off in the car towards Chianciano and then hesitated.

Was he just being a drama queen? Maybe she was just taking time out, doing what she always did?

The chestnut woods. Of course.

He'd check on the way. It wouldn't take him far off his route, and it would be stupid to go so far if that was all she was doing.

He skidded down the track and found her car immediately, parked by the side of the track near where they'd had their picnic the other week. It wasn't locked, and her bag was in it, her phone inside, with all its missed calls and voicemail messages from him. Still worried half to death, ready to kill her, he forced himself to walk towards the clearing.

And there she was, sitting on the ground under the tree he'd fallen out of as a child, and she turned her head and smiled at him and he thought he was going to be sick with relief.

'*Ciao,* Gio. I knew you'd find me. I've hurt my ankle.'

Thank God. He'd been so afraid—

'It probably wouldn't have killed you to have your phone on you,' he said gruffly, dropping it in her lap before sitting down beside her and pulling her into his arms.

'I left it in the car. Have you been trying to get me? I could hear it ringing, but I couldn't get there. I'm sorry.'

'Don't be. What have you done to your ankle?'

She shrugged. 'Just twisted it. I must have stood on a root or something, and it just turned under me, but I can't put any weight on it.' She rested her head against his shoulder. 'I'm sorry I worried you. I knew you'd know where to find me.'

'Only because I drove past the end of the track. I was going to Chianciano to look for you.'

'Ah. I walked out of the meeting. The bride was being unrealistic and stroppy, and I didn't need to have that sort of hassle, so I did what you suggested and cherry-picked her out of my life. Then I came here to think, and I've had rather more time to do it than I anticipated. Still, it's been useful. I've got lots to tell you.'

'I've got lots to tell you, too. Can I go first?'

'Sure. Just let me get these messages. They can't all be from you.'

'They might well be,' he said drily, and she bit her lip guiltily.

She started to listen to them, and one after the other, they grew more desperate, until by the last one she could tell he was coming unravelled.

Anita, please call me! I don't know where you are, and I think something must have happened. Please, call me, cara. I love you.

She stared at the phone. Did he mean it?

'Did you mean it?'

'What?'

'You said you love me.'

He smiled ruefully and brushed his knuckles over her cheek. 'Yes, *cara*, I meant it. *Te amo*, Anita. I love you. That's what I was coming home to tell you.'

'Oh, Gio!'

She burst into tears and flung her arms around him, sobbing. 'You have no idea how long I've waited to hear you say that,' she mumbled into his shirt, and he gathered her up against his chest and held her while she cried.

'I'm sorry,' she said, pulling herself together with an effort and tilting her head so she could see his face.

His eyes were tender, bright with tears, and he brushed the hair back from her face and kissed her slowly.

'I love you,' he said quietly. 'I think I've probably always loved you. That's why I've never been able to love anyone else, because none of them were you. I should have talked to you years ago, told you how I felt, but I didn't really understand it until now, when I couldn't find you. I knew I loved you—I'd realised that this morning while I was packing up some things in my apartment, but it was only when I couldn't get hold of you and I started to think of all the dreadful things that could have happened—'

'Shh,' she murmured, pulling his face down and kissing him gently. 'I'm sorry. I'm so, so sorry.'

'It's all right. It doesn't matter now.'

He let her go, to her regret, and got up—only he didn't, not really. He went up onto his knees, then bent one leg up so the foot was on the ground, and then he took her hand. On one knee?

'Gio?' she said softly, and he smiled.

'Marry me, Anita,' he said quietly. 'I know I've been an

idiot. I should have talked to you long ago, worked it out, because it's so blindingly obvious to me now, but I just didn't realise how much you meant to me, and I had no idea what happiness truly was until now. In fact it's such a recent revelation I haven't even got you a ring, but you're a difficult woman to please and I'm sure you'll have your own ideas,' he added with a smile.

'So, will you? Please? Marry me, and let me love you and look after you and our baby, and make a life for us, here in the country surrounded by our families?'

'Oh, Gio! Of course I will. I'd love to marry you,' she said, tears welling in her eyes, and he pulled her into his arms and kissed her as if she was the most precious thing in the universe.

Then he eased away, looking down into her face and wiping away a tear with his thumb. 'Come on, let's get you home and sort this ankle out.'

He scooped her up and put her in his car, and she sent him back to fetch her shopping and her bag, and then he drove her home, carried her inside and looked at her ankle.

'Do you think it needs hospital?' he asked, and she shook her head.

'No. We could ask Luca to look at it, but later. Stick some ice on it and come and sit down and let me tell you what I've been thinking.'

'Let me guess,' he said, sealing crushed ice in a bag and wrapping it in a towel before placing it gently on her foot. 'You want to ditch your business.'

'No, but I do want to scale it back, at least until the baby's older. How did you know?'

He smiled. 'Because I've spent the last few days planning how to scale back mine.'

Her eyes widened. 'You're closing your law practice?'

'Not entirely. I'm going into the family business, but I might keep a small amount of work going, maybe more locally. I'm sick of it, Nita. I've done nothing else for too long, and now it's time to come home, to the things that really matter. You, the baby, my family.'

He hadn't called her Nita for years, not since they'd been children, and it made her want to cry with happiness.

He looked down at her hand, stroking her ring finger. 'Just one thing,' he said, 'before you go off on maternity leave. I've got a job for you. How quickly can you arrange a wedding?'

She laughed. 'Oh, Gio, you'd be amazed.'

'Good. Because I've discovered that the idea of having you as my wife is getting more and more appealing, and I've realised I don't want to wait any longer than I absolutely have to.'

'Can you give me four weeks?'

'If I must. Can you organise the sort of wedding you want in that time?'

She laughed, the musical sound filling him with joy. 'Oh, Gio, of course I can. I've been planning it in my head since I was fourteen years old. I know *exactly* what I want.'

'Well, we'd better make sure you have it, then.'

They were married in the chapel in the *palazzo* five weeks later.

It took a little longer than she'd thought because they had to stop planning every few minutes to hug and kiss and talk some more. Highly distracting, but she wouldn't have changed it for the world.

She'd spent years now creating dream weddings for other people, and she knew exactly how to achieve what she wanted. It wasn't complicated.

No hoopla, no nonsense, no fireworks or star-studded ceilings in a marquee, no entertainment or extravagance.

Just the people they loved. Their family and friends, gathered round to celebrate their union, and she had her wish.

It was a glorious day. She wore a simple lace dress that fitted her beautifully and proudly showed off her baby bump, and an ancient lace veil that had belonged to her great-grandmother, and Lydia and Carlotta cooked the most amazing wedding breakfast. They set up tables in the colonnaded courtyard in the *palazzo,* and after they'd eaten they cleared them away and had dancing.

And then, when she began to flag, Gio scooped her up in his arms and carried her down the steps of the *palazzo* to the waiting car, and they were driven away.

Not home, not that first night, because the builders were in, but to the bridal suite of a nearby hotel.

She was still in her wedding dress, and they shed confetti all the way up stairs to their room, but nobody minded. They were well known in the area, and well loved, and it was a wedding they'd all been looking forward to for years.

Gio closed the door behind them, and drew her into his arms. She was still smiling. She'd been smiling that morning when she got up in her parents' home for the last time as a single woman, and she'd smiled all day.

'Happy?' he murmured.

'Very happy. You?'

He nodded, his eyes caressing her. 'Of course. How could I be anything else? I've got the most wonderful wife in the world, we're having a baby—life's perfect.' He bent his head and kissed her.

'*Te amo,* Anita. *Te amo...*'

* * *

Four and a half months later, at the end of October and right in the middle of harvest, Anita gave birth to his son.

He was born in the morning, and by evening he was at home with them, the crib all ready beside their bed, and after she'd fed him Gio changed his nappy, a little nervously despite all the practice on his nieces and nephews, and then settled down beside her, the baby cradled in his arms.

She rested her head on his shoulder, and he smiled down at her. 'OK?'

'Definitely. I'm glad he wasn't too early. I can still smell the paint.'

Gio laughed softly. 'The poor builders. They've been here all day clearing up the last of their mess, but at least he's got a nursery when he needs it, even if he hasn't got a name.'

'We'll choose one.'

'He might have to have two. How about Luigi?'

'No. How about Mario?'

'What, as in Super Mario?'

She laughed and snuggled closer. 'How about we put all the names in a pot and pull one out and call him that?'

He stared down at his baby, a tiny frown between his eyebrows as he stroked his fingers tenderly over his son's soft, downy cheek. 'Or we could call him Georgio, after Camilla's son. After all, in a distorted sort of way we owe him for all this. Without him, she wouldn't have been in that situation, and without us being thrown together we might never have come to our senses.'

'We?' She tilted her head round so she could see his face, and laughed at him, but not unkindly. 'I never lost my senses. I've been in love with you since I was tiny, and I've always known it. You're the one who came to his senses, and you certainly took your time.'

He hugged her with his free arm, snuggling her closer, holding the people he loved most in the world against his heart. How could he ever have doubted that he loved this wonderful, brave, generous woman who'd been his life-long companion and friend? He'd fought it for years, failed Kirsten not because she wasn't loveable but because his heart was already taken. He just hadn't admitted it, but there was no denying it now, and he bent his head and pressed a tender kiss to her lips.

'Well, at least you know it wasn't a hasty decision. So—Georgio?'

She nodded slowly. 'Yes. I like it, and I like the idea of calling our baby after him.' She gazed down at their baby, perfect in every way, and felt a wave of love so strong she had to blink away the tears.

'He's beautiful,' Gio said softly, and rested his cheek against her forehead. 'Just like his mother. Did I ever mention that I love you, Anita Valtieri?'

'I'm not sure. Say it again, just in case?'

She felt his smile, then the soft graze of stubble as he turned his head and kissed her tenderly.

'Te amo, carissima. Te amo...'

* * * * *

Mills & Boon® Hardback

September 2012

ROMANCE

Unlocking her Innocence	Lynne Graham
Santiago's Command	Kim Lawrence
His Reputation Precedes Him	Carole Mortimer
The Price of Retribution	Sara Craven
Just One Last Night	Helen Brooks
The Greek's Acquisition	Chantelle Shaw
The Husband She Never Knew	Kate Hewitt
When Only Diamonds Will Do	Lindsay Armstrong
The Couple Behind the Headlines	Lucy King
The Best Mistake of Her Life	Aimee Carson
The Valtieri Baby	Caroline Anderson
Slow Dance with the Sheriff	Nikki Logan
Bella's Impossible Boss	Michelle Douglas
The Tycoon's Secret Daughter	Susan Meier
She's So Over Him	Joss Wood
Return of the Last McKenna	Shirley Jump
Once a Playboy...	Kate Hardy
Challenging the Nurse's Rules	Janice Lynn

MEDICAL

Her Motherhood Wish	Anne Fraser
A Bond Between Strangers	Scarlet Wilson
The Sheikh and the Surrogate Mum	Meredith Webber
Tamed by her Brooding Boss	Joanna Neil

0812 GEN STD HB

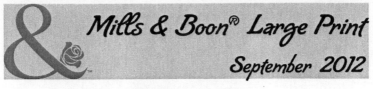

Mills & Boon® Large Print

September 2012

ROMANCE

HISTORICAL

MEDICAL

ROMANCE

Banished to the Harem	Carol Marinelli
Not Just the Greek's Wife	Lucy Monroe
A Delicious Deception	Elizabeth Power
Painted the Other Woman	Julia James
A Game of Vows	Maisey Yates
A Devil in Disguise	Caitlin Crews
Revelations of the Night Before	Lynn Raye Harris
Defying her Desert Duty	Annie West
The Wedding Must Go On	Robyn Grady
The Devil and the Deep	Amy Andrews
Taming the Brooding Cattleman	Marion Lennox
The Rancher's Unexpected Family	Myrna Mackenzie
Single Dad's Holiday Wedding	Patricia Thayer
Nanny for the Millionaire's Twins	Susan Meier
Truth-Or-Date.com	Nina Harrington
Wedding Date with Mr Wrong	Nicola Marsh
The Family Who Made Him Whole	Jennifer Taylor
The Doctor Meets Her Match	Annie Claydon

MEDICAL

A Socialite's Christmas Wish	Lucy Clark
Redeeming Dr Riccardi	Leah Martyn
The Doctor's Lost-and-Found Heart	Dianne Drake
The Man Who Wouldn't Marry	Tina Beckett

Mills & Boon® Large Print

October 2012

ROMANCE

A Secret Disgrace	Penny Jordan
The Dark Side of Desire	Julia James
The Forbidden Ferrara	Sarah Morgan
The Truth Behind his Touch	Cathy Williams
Plain Jane in the Spotlight	Lucy Gordon
Battle for the Soldier's Heart	Cara Colter
The Navy SEAL's Bride	Soraya Lane
My Greek Island Fling	Nina Harrington
Enemies at the Altar	Melanie Milburne
In the Italian's Sights	Helen Brooks
In Defiance of Duty	Caitlin Crews

HISTORICAL

The Duchess Hunt	Elizabeth Beacon
Marriage of Mercy	Carla Kelly
Unbuttoning Miss Hardwick	Deb Marlowe
Chained to the Barbarian	Carol Townend
My Fair Concubine	Jeannie Lin

MEDICAL

Georgie's Big Greek Wedding?	Emily Forbes
The Nurse's Not-So-Secret Scandal	Wendy S. Marcus
Dr Right All Along	Joanna Neil
Summer With A French Surgeon	Margaret Barker
Sydney Harbour Hospital: Tom's Redemption	Fiona Lowe
Doctor on Her Doorstep	Annie Claydon